SO-BJO-923

The Winds of Mars

THE
WINDS of MARS

by H. M. HOOVER

DUTTON CHILDREN'S BOOKS • NEW YORK

Copyright © 1995 by H. M. Hoover

All rights reserved. No part of this publication may be reproduced or transmitted in any form or by any means, electronic or mechanical, including photocopy, recording, or any information storage and retrieval system now known or to be invented, without permission in writing from the publisher, except by a reviewer who wishes to quote brief passages in connection with a review written for inclusion in a magazine, newspaper, or broadcast.

Library of Congress Cataloging-in-Publication Data
Hoover, H. M.
The winds of Mars / by H. M. Hoover.—1st ed.   p.   cm.
Summary: When rebel forces strike against her father, the all-powerful president of Mars, teenage Annalyn finds her comfortable existence turned upside down and her life threatened from unexpected sources.
ISBN 0-525-45359-8
[1. Science fiction.]   I. Title.
PZ7.H7705Wi 1995   [Fic]—dc20 94-32095 CIP AC

Published in the United States by Dutton Children's Books,
a division of Penguin Books USA Inc.
375 Hudson Street, New York, New York 10014

Editor: Ann Durell   Designer: Semadar Megged
Printed in USA   First Edition
10 9 8 7 6 5 4 3 2 1

The Winds of Mars

1

JUST FOR THE RECORD, MY NAME IS ANNALYN
Reynolds Court. I'm five feet four inches tall, weigh fifty
pounds, and am seventeen Earth-years old. My hair is
brown and thick and curly. I usually wear it short, but
it's growing out here and doesn't look too bad. My eyes
are brown, my nose is straight, and so far I don't wear
makeup.

I feel awkward recording this. But if I tell it as a story,
maybe that will help me understand what happened—
how one thing led to the next. My problem is remembering, and deciding which memories really matter.

The most important thing is, I guess . . . I'm the legal
daughter of Charles Reynolds, the President of Mars, and
Ingrid Court, the commander of a star-probe vessel. She
and her ship left Mars orbit a few months after I was
born. That's all I know about her—and I learned that
from gossip and old files. No one ever talked about her,
at least not to me.

I was born in the capital city of Olympia. Cities here
are all built inside old volcano craters to protect them
from sandstorms, then covered with domes or shields
filled with Earth-like atmosphere. Olympia is in one of
the deepest craters.

From the air, the city's shields look like crystal clusters sticking up out of the sand. Light makes the crystals sparkle. City lights are always on; Mars is so far from the sun that our brightest day is twilight.

Olympia has five major shields. The largest, in the center of the crater, covers Midtown, where the common techs and service people live. A forested park called the Greenway links Midtown to the zoo and botanical garden shield. Then there's the spaceport, the Agricultural Center, and The Fountains. Seven smaller shields covered the hotels and the convention center.

The Fountains' shield stood in the most protected part of the crater and sparkled like a giant yellow diamond. It was named for Fountain House, the presidential palace, which it sheltered, along with the military academy, federal courts, and the Council Building. Council members had their homes there, as did the most important diplomats. The grounds were lush with trees, formal gardens, fountains, and reflecting pools.

One wing of Fountain House was separate from the rest. Called the Sanctuary, it's where the President's family lived—where I lived as a child.

I was raised by servants. My mother was gone. And although my father lived a short walk away, the only time I saw him was on a news broadcast. Evan, my half-brother, said he'd met him once when he was small but couldn't remember much about him except that the President had patted him on the head and it hurt.

Evan lived with his mother, Janis Parker, the President's last wife. Janis was—is—tall, pale blond . . . beautiful. I always think of her in ice blue. She wore that color often—to match her eyes—and long blue crystal earrings. I was afraid of her, maybe because I knew she didn't like me.

Janis was in charge of the Sanctuary, and she was a tyrant. She always expected everything to look perfect. She yelled at the servants, at Evan, at me. She would even yell at robocleaners—which made people laugh at her behind her back. As the older children moved out, the empty apartments were offered to retired members of the presidential staff. Most turned them down, not wanting to put up with her.

I remember one day when I was small, Shala—my nurse-companion—and I were going to the zoo. Evan saw us leaving and wanted to go along. He said his mother was lunching with the President and wouldn't mind.

Shala said he had to leave a message for Janis, so she'd know where he was and when he would be back. Evan refused, saying he was no baby who had to explain where he went. "Then you can't go," Shala said.

But I wanted him to come, so I ran back across the big courtyard to his apartment and told their house computer. That was a mistake.

We were eating cotton candy and looking at the bears when we heard sirens. A yellow zoo security van, lights flashing, nosed its way through the crowded walkway. Before it came to a stop beside us, Janis jumped from the cab. As soon as I saw her I knew we were in trouble, but I didn't know why. The driver got out slowly, looking upset.

"Annalyn Court!" Janis's outraged shout startled the bears and made my knees go weak. "How dare you enter my apartment when I'm out? I come home to find my son missing! Possibly kidnapped! The President's son! I call the guards—and they find your voice on my computer!"

And on and on she went, shouting down my and Shala's intimidated attempts to explain. Until Evan, who'd gone to her at once to pat her arm and try to calm her down, finally said, "Everyone's staring at you, Mother."

She glanced around, saw it was true, and turned to slide open the van's side door. Inside was an animal cage. "Get in there," she ordered. "We're going home. Evan, sit in front with me."

I looked up at Shala. She was almost in tears, clutching her cotton candy stick so hard her knuckles were white. No servant could talk back to an elite. But I could.

"No!" I told Janis. "You can't make us!" I was scared, but I wasn't going to let Shala be shamed by being forced into that cage. "Evan asked to come along. He said you wouldn't mind. Tell her, Evan."

"That's typical of you, Annalyn, trying to blame him!"

"It's the truth! And you know it, Evan!" That's the

only time I ever heard Shala's voice raised in anger. She glared at Evan until he finally spoke up.

"It's not Annie's fault, Mother. She's just a little kid. Please! Can we go now? People are looking at us."

And they were. A few with undisguised contempt. Janis had been recognized; her name was being whispered among the crowd. Some smiled to see the First Lady making a scene; most looked at Shala and me with pity; others almost tiptoed away.

"Mother!"

As Janis hesitated, Evan burst into loud, theatrical tears. To keep commoners from seeing her son cry, she half-lifted him into the front seat and slid in after him, telling the guard, "Get us out of here! What are you waiting for? Drive!" Her parting words to me were: "You just wait."

The outing was ruined, but we took our time going home, afraid of what Janis might do.

I was sure she'd never allow Evan to play with me again, and that made me very sad. He was not only my big, worldly half-brother; I worshipped him. Anything Evan said or did was law to me.

To my great relief, Evan came over to have breakfast with us as usual the next morning. Janis always slept late. He said his mother was still mad at me, but he could handle her.

Remembering her threat, I waited for a long time, but nothing bad happened to me—that I actually could blame on Janis, that is.

Shala Parvez was, in every way that matters, my mother. My first memories are of her. She was never anything but good to me, and I loved and trusted her completely.

She was only fifteen when she was assigned to me. Two years younger than I am now. Her parents were starfleet crewmem who left their baby behind on Mars when they returned to space. Like my mother. Maybe that's why she took such good care of me.

Like all starfleet children, she was made a ward of the state and raised in the federal training school in the city of Regis. After their primary education, most wards become tech apprentices; some become crewmem like their parents. Shala had no interest in technical things. She wanted to work with people. At the school she had always looked after the smaller children. By choice, not assignment.

She took me with her once when she went back to visit her school. It was plain she was a favorite with both the students and the staff. I came home feeling especially lucky to have her.

Small and quick and bright, Shala had curly black hair and a wonderful laugh. She was soft-spoken and gentle. Evan always envied me because of her—he once admitted he wished she was his mother. She loved music and taught me how to whistle and sing and play the guitar. Her dream—after I grew up and no longer needed her—was to have a café where people would come to eat and play and sing and enjoy themselves with her.

Now that I think about it, she was probably lonely living at the Sanctuary. I was. After visiting her old school I remember wishing she and I could live *there*.

We shared everything, the same luxury apartment, the same easy life. We even shared my studies sometimes, until she got bored.

The thing is, I like learning just for the fun of knowing. For example, when Shala began teaching me the guitar, I wanted to know all about guitars; who invented them and who wrote the first music. Shala told me all she knew, so then I asked the computer, and it told me lots more interesting things—much more than Shala wanted to know.

But she saw that I liked learning and she talked with Mr. Koh, who headed The Fountains school, and had him set up lessons for me until I was old enough to go to school.

There were less than a hundred students in The Fountains school. Some were Council members' children, but most came from diplomatic families. We didn't have classes. Each of us learned at his or her own pace; tutors helped, if needed.

Most of us could have learned as well at home; the main purpose of the school was to teach us to get along with other people . . . elite people.

Evan wasn't a good student. He was often in trouble with Mr. Koh. He had a quick temper, and when he got bored studying—impatience gave him a short attention span—he couldn't resist the urge to liven things up with tricks and practical jokes. At rec time, he usually chose the games we'd play. When sides were chosen, he was always one of the first kids picked.

I was always the last to be chosen if Evan wasn't a captain. Not only was I one of the youngest students, but the tutors and Mr. Koh called me "gifted." They would tell the other kids they could be more like me "if only you apply yourself," which made kids resent me.

Evan told me that. I asked him once why I wasn't more popular. "Don't you know?" he said, and told me, adding, "you're too smart, Annie. You make people nervous. You talk like a grown-up. Kids would like you better if you were quiet. And didn't study so much. Try it and see."

I promised I would and thanked him for being so honest.

When Mr. Koh noticed a difference in my schoolwork, he spoke to Shala—who talked to me. When I told her what Evan said, and how he always tried to help me, she got very quiet.

Finally she spoke. "Evan may mean well, and want you to be popular. But he's not old enough to understand he's done a bad thing by asking you to pretend to be less than you are. You are gifted; to waste that gift is to spit in God's eye."

I understood what Shala was saying, but I thought she didn't understand what school was like. Still, pretending to be less smart hadn't helped. Now the kids thought I was really boring. So I went back to studying as much as I wanted, but didn't talk as much. That seemed to please Evan.

Even though he was a year older, I could have graduated two years before he did. Instead, I was held back —because of my age, Janis told Shala. The two of us entered the military academy together.

2

CADETS HAD TO LIVE AT THE ACADEMY. WHEN I
started to school there, I had to say good-bye not only to
Shala, but also to the only home I'd ever known. Our
apartment in the Sanctuary would be given to someone
else.

With her responsibility to me ended, Shala was moving to Midtown to complete her own education. She
would study hotel management, she said, and get a good
job and save her salary so that sometime she could afford
to open her own café.

Leaving Shala was the hardest thing I'd ever had to
do. We both cried for days every time we thought about
it. When she left me in the academy commandant's office,
to my great embarrassment I burst into tears again.

My interview with the commandant, General Offrey,
was brief—once I quit crying. He was basically kind. All
he said about my crying was: "Think how much sadder
it would be if you were glad to see her go." Then he said
with my IQ and scholastic record he expected a lot from
me. I sniffed and promised to try to live up to his ex-
pectations.

"My aide will show you to your quarters."

The aide led me up ramps, around corners, down halls, and left me at the door to my new room. It was a small box furnished in Early Institutional with a desk-computer, locker, two chairs, a bed, my guitar, and a box of personal belongings.

Through an open door was your basic sanit. I remember being disappointed there was no tub, only a shower. I didn't learn for years that the only apartments on Mars with the luxury of real bathrooms—with tubs—were those in Fountain House.

I was still standing there when the door across the hall slid open and Evan came out. To my surprise he was already wearing a green cadet uniform. He gave me a swift, appraising glance—then realized it was me and his mouth fell open.

"Annie!" He hugged me as if we hadn't met in years instead of the morning before. "Finally a friendly face. The people here are robots, all stiff and correct. You have to—"

"When did you get here? We weren't supposed to check in until three—"

"Oh—uh. Yesterday. You know Mother. She thought because she's First Lady, her son should be first here." He made a face, and grinned. "Like it matters."

"You didn't say anything at breakfast yesterday."

"I forgot. Come on. Let's go down to supply and get your uniforms and boots and stuff."

That was how these last five years of my life began. In a way, they turned out to be my happiest years. In

spite of the fact that I cried myself to sleep the first few
nights because I missed Shala and my own room and my
own bed.

Sleep ended abruptly my first morning at the academy. I was grabbed by the shoulder, yanked out of bed,
and stood on the carpet. By the time I got my eyes open
I was nose to nose with a brass buckle, then I was turned
sideways so that I might see the time. It was six in the
morning.

"You're a cadet now," said a firm female voice. "Not
a pampered child. Wake-up is 5 A.M. Didn't you hear the
chimes?"

They had wakened me, but I had ignored them as
rude noises in the middle of the night. There were no
wake-up signals in the Sanctuary. "Is Evan up?" I said,
wondering if he'd known about the chimes and, if so,
why he hadn't wakened me. My tormenter didn't
answer.

She was tall and muscular, dressed in a sergeant's
blue tunic, black tights and boots. A laser scar traced a
shiny red line from her neat brown hair down her left
cheek and under her jaw. I wondered how she got that
and how much it had hurt.

"I'm Kati Assam, your mentor. Your father appreci-
ates my skills so much that he appointed me to teach his
children discipline. I've never disappointed the President.
I won't allow you to disappoint either of us. Now use the
sanit and get dressed."

She freed me with a little push and I stumbled into
my military career, heart racing.

"You missed breakfast and wake-up calisthenics, but I'll find something to give you an adequate exercise." Her teeth were white against her dark skin as she grinned down at me. "Some of our cleaning drones are down for repairs."

After a stop at a food server for a sandwich and juice, I spent my first day as a cadet guiding a vacuum cleaner over the blue carpet and endless rows of green seats in an empty auditorium, then polishing all the metal trim—and hating Sergeant Assam.

It had never occurred to me that humans might do manual labor. I felt it was a personal insult and Sergeant Assam was a sadist. If this was what my father expected me to do, who cared if he never bothered to come and see me? If Shala knew what I was doing now . . . she couldn't do anything about it. I was on my own. That was a scary—if important—thought.

Lunchtime came and went; no one came to get me. Full of resentment, I decided to do the best job that had ever been done. I'd show that Kati Assam!

My only rest breaks were trips to the sanit and the water fountains. My hands developed blisters; my back and arms began to ache. Several times I almost cried in self-pity, but I kept on working. By late afternoon the place was spotless—and I was sure she'd forgotten all about me.

When Sergeant Assam finally came back she silently inspected my work, row by row. Then, to my relief, she smiled and said, "Well done, cadet. This was a character test. All new cadets experience them. Each is given an equally unpleasant task and observed as they work. Plainly you were born with, or were taught, a sense of responsibility. Faced with thankless drudgery, you still did your best. I'm pleased with you."

"I missed lunch," I said, hoping my sacrifice would add to her good opinion.

"There's no lunch. Cadets eat twice a day, breakfast and dinner. You would have learned that at breakfast, had you bothered to get up. You would also know that we shower and dress for dinner. You will do that now. You will pick up your class schedule when you leave the dining room. Regular classes begin tomorrow. You will rise at the sound of the chimes."

"May I ask a question?"

"Yes."

"How do I find my room?"

3

EAGER TO KNOW WHAT TERRIBLE JOB EVAN HAD been assigned that day, I knocked on his door. When he didn't answer, I assumed he'd gone on up to dinner.

Located in the penthouse, the dining room was a glass-enclosed half-circle. From any point in the room you could see the frost-tipped bulk of Nix Olympica, distorted by the crystal shield, rising up into the sky beyond the crater rim.

Seating was assigned. At my table were officers and senior cadets. My heart sank when I saw my place was right next to Sergeant Assam, but she was surprisingly gracious, making me feel welcome, introducing me to everyone.

Two of the cadets turned out to be my half-sisters. I didn't know them at all, but they remembered me as a little kid in the Sanctuary. "You were always singing," one said. "When she wasn't climbing into the courtyard fountain," said the other. Both seemed nice.

The menu was roast beef, salad, and lemon cake for dessert. Food never tasted better. The others discussed vacation trips to various habitats, Earth, and her moon, Luna. I ate and listened. It was interesting—especially to someone as sheltered as I was. Except for one trip to the city of Regis, the only traveling I'd ever done was to the zoo and the botanical gardens. There was no reason for Shala to take me anywhere else, and considering whose child I was, maybe she was forbidden to for fear of kidnapping.

When I felt less shy I looked around for Evan. Sergeant Assam asked who I was hunting for.

"He's assigned to this table," she said, "but he's spending tonight on the Green, without dinner. It's hoped the time and solitude out there will help him understand he must learn to control his temper and correct his manners."

It sounded as if Evan had flunked his character test.

When no one was looking, I tucked some of the meat in a roll, wrapped it in my napkin with carrot sticks and cake, and tucked the packet under my tunic. After dinner, I remembered to pick up my schedule and then got a juice cube from the cooler in the lobby.

When the door to the Green closed behind me I couldn't see a thing. The arcade and fountain lights were off. Privacy shades in the windows shut off the lights from the buildings. It was so dark the blur of stars was visible through the shield.

I'd never been in such a dark space and instantly understood why being sent out here at night was punishment.

"Annie? Wait there," Evan called. He'd seen me in the light from the hall door. I heard him running across the lawn and then his hand touched my arm. "You shouldn't be out here," he said. "I'm supposed to be in solitary. I don't want you to get in trouble, too."

"I brought you a sandwich."

"Thanks! I'm starved. Who told you where I was?"

"Sergeant Assam." I heard him take a bite of sandwich.

"They were all talking about me!"

"No."

"Oh." He seemed disappointed. "You'd better go back."

"Not until you tell me why you're out here."

"I said something Assam didn't like." He started walking and I followed. "I don't care if she works for the President," he burst out. "She's just a sergeant, a commoner. But I'm his son. I'll play the game now, to get along, but when I get out of here, she's going to be sorry."

Reaching the fountain, he sat down and leaned back against the stone. I sat down beside him—and discovered every muscle in my body was starting to ache from all that cleaning. The grass smelled good, but the ground was so cold I shivered.

"What did you say to her?" I persisted.

"She told me to do a stupid job. I refused. We got into an argument . . . and I told her she was going to die."

I wasn't sure I understood. "You threatened to kill her?"

"No," he said, impatiently. "I said she was going to die—and I hoped it was soon. It was stupid of me and I shouldn't have said it. What if they tell Mother?"

I thought that over. "She'll be upset because you got in trouble the first day, but she always forgives you. What you said was out of line, but not that bad—everybody dies."

"Not us. Not important people. We don't die," said Evan. Darkness kept me from seeing his face, but an angry note of resentment entered his voice at my laugh of disbelief. "It's true! Don't laugh. You just don't know any better. Mother only told me because . . . she thought I should know."

"But that's impossible. How could Janis believe she'll live forever?"

"Not just her. Us. Me and you and some other people."

"Why does she think that?"

"You have to promise not to tell."

"I promise." I was wondering to whom he thought I would repeat something so incredible, and also if his mother's rages were symptoms of a serious mental problem.

"No. I mean *really* promise." He was emphatic. "It's important. You can't tell anyone. Ever. Not even Shala."

I promised.

"When you're born," he said, "if your parents are very important, they have doctors bury a tiny mind-transfer chip deep inside your head." Evan was almost whispering even though we were completely alone. "It records everything that goes through your brain. Everything you think and feel and eat and do. Even when you pee and stuff. All this data is transmitted to a central storage unit. Then, when your body wears out, they have an android body ready that looks just like you. And the mind the computer saved is loaded into the android. So you never really die," he added triumphantly.

As he talked I became more and more horrified. I didn't want to believe him, although I instinctively felt it was true. Evan wouldn't lie to me, even as a joke. And Janis wouldn't have told her son such a fantastic lie.

"Say something, Annie. Don't just sit there." He sounded scared. Which scared me.

At that moment I was sure I could feel it, a hard little kernel of cold deep in my brain, right at the base of my skull. I wanted to vomit.

"All his kids have them," he went on, still trying to convince me. "That's why Mother made him give her one before she'd marry him—to make him prove she was as important to him as his children. She says he was one of the first people to ever have one—that he's so old he's had at least four different android bodies."

That was too much to believe. "Now I know you're putting me on," I said. "If he was an android, he couldn't be our father. Androids are machines. They can't have children."

"He can," said Evan.

"Besides," I went on, "he's *real*. When you see him in his car, or when he's on the news—you can see he's real."

"They all *look* real, Annie." He seemed so sure, and amused by my reaction. "Nobody *looks* like an android. Nobody would want to be around them if they knew."

"My father is real! He is! You can't make me believe this!"

"Be quiet! Stop it!" I tried to get up, but Evan pulled me back down onto the stone where we were sitting. I wanted to run away, but there was no way to escape something inside my head.

"Calm down! You don't want them to know you're out here." He held on to my wrist with both hands and all his weight. "I was kidding, Annie. Joking. Don't you know a story when you hear one?"

"Are you saying that was all a lie?" I had to know. I couldn't bear to think I had a computer chip in my brain, spying on me constantly. Computers could be accessed; who else might know my thoughts? "Tell me now! Were you lying?"

"Shut up!" he whispered desperately. "I was kidding."

"You sounded like you meant it."

"Would you have believed me if I hadn't? How else could I trick you?"

"If that's your idea of a joke, you're sick!" I said.

We were both quiet for a bit; I regaining my composure and Evan still holding on to me in case I panicked again.

"I didn't mean to scare you, Annie," he said after a time, "but what's so terrible about the idea? Wouldn't you like to live forever? To travel as far as you want to in space? We could be friends forever. Really *forever*."

"I'd hate knowing I wasn't me—just a computer copy. Never knowing if I really thought or felt anything, or if it was all just simulation. And what would happen if someone erased your mind?"

"They make copies . . . I mean, they could." He corrected himself. "And put the copies in different places, all secure."

"Where?"

"I don't know." He let go of my arm and got up, tired of our discussion. "The juice made me cold. I have to jog to keep warm. You should go in before we both get caught. It was just one of my famous stupid jokes. OK? Forget about it. You've got no sense of humor."

He pulled me to my feet and we started toward the door. "But just in case," he said then, "don't tell anybody about this. If my mother found out I . . . made up a story like this, she'd kill me. Promise?"

"Could you be killed, Evan?" I wanted an honest answer.

"Sure," he said, and laughed, "so long as you make sure all my copies are destroyed."

4

THAT NIGHT IN THE SHOWER I SEARCHED MY WET head for a lump. Nothing. I looked down my throat with a magnifying mirror. Disgusting but normal. I don't know what I expected to find, but not finding anything didn't make me feel better.

The second day at the academy was better than the first. This time the chimes really woke me. Scared of being late, I jumped up and nearly fell, my muscles were so sore. At the morning exercises, along with half the other new cadets, I couldn't help groaning at every move.

We all began to giggle. The groans got louder. The laughter spread until Sergeant Assam got angry. "No wonder the Earth-born call us weaklings," she said.

"Earthies are just jealous because they're too poor to buy robots to do their work," Evan said loud enough for her to hear. "They have to be strong. We don't."

"No cadet becomes an officer without completing surface training, Cadet Parker," said the sergeant. "Perhaps your mother will buy you a robot to carry you around in your pressure suit when you must go outside the shields. Without physical strength you'll die out there. It's up to you, of course."

Some cadets laughed. Evan got red-faced with anger

but didn't answer back. I figured he didn't want to risk spending another night on the Green.

After breakfast we went to our first lecture—in the same auditorium I'd cleaned. Our class filled only the first three rows. General Offrey was our speaker.

"You are all privileged young citizens," he began. "That's why you're here. Because you are privileged, you owe society something in return."

That was a new idea to most of us.

"Mars, like Earth's moon," he went on, "was colonized by corporate investors to manufacture products they couldn't make on Earth, either because of gravity, or pollution, or—most importantly—because they wanted to develop technology in secret.

"One business in particular made Mars rich and powerful—advanced nanotechnology. Molecular assembling machines, or as you no doubt call them, our 'tiny robots.'

"For security, the assembler factories were built deep under the planet's surface in laser-hollowed chambers. Down there in the darkness are endless tanks of nutrient soup. Raw material is piped in; finished goods come out. You'll be taken down to those chambers on field trips.

"Assemblers built the sapphire crystal shields that cover our cities. Sandstorms blasting against a shield at three-hundred-plus miles an hour for a month or more can do a lot of damage. Assemblers work continuously to make repairs."

There was a murmur of excited whispers. Hands went up. Many of us hadn't known the shields were vulnerable and were frightened by the idea. The general said to save all our questions until he was finished.

"Assembler robots can duplicate almost anything," he continued, "atom by atom. All the protein you eat, the clothes you wear, the seats you're occupying, were made by them. They can make a pressure suit, or a golf club, or the parts of a landcar or aircar, or a spaceship. All they need to create is raw material, a seed or 'template,' and time.

"Speaking of time, in years to come you'll probably use a special type of assembler for a rejuv fix to keep looking as young and healthy as you look today.

"Since much of the raw material the assemblers use comes from waste products, our factories are very profitable.

"More than a century ago, our wealth enabled us to declare our independence from foreign corporate rule. Our wealth attracts envy, and danger, from aggressive outsiders. That's where you come into the picture.

"We've been called imperial, greedy, and betrayers of humankind's hope—and those are the nicer things. The truth is, we Martians are guilty of nothing more than keeping for ourselves what thousands of our ancestors died to create.

"To protect ourselves from any foreign intervention, we developed an automated defense system. It works equally well against spaceships or asteroids.

"Academy graduates aren't military officers in the old historical sense. You'll never have to go into battle, or lead armies. No enemy will get that close. Your training will help you provide the human link between our computers and our defense system.

"Some of you will serve the President and Council in a variety of duties, many of them diplomatic. Others will become intelligence experts. A few will provide personal security for our President. Whatever your eventual individual assignments may be, by helping keep Mars secure, you will benefit and protect all of its people."

I was stiffling a yawn when Sergeant Assam tapped me on the shoulder and motioned for me to get up and follow her out. I went, wondering if I was in trouble for yawning.

"There's a woman to see you in the visitors' lounge," she said when we reached the lobby. "I wouldn't have interrupted you but she has to catch a noon shuttle."

"Who is it?"

Assam shrugged. "Someone with top security clearance and the influence to match. That's all I know. Now hurry."

The woman pacing restlessly in the lounge wore a navy blue uniform I didn't recognize. She was probably in her early thirties, older than Shala. Her face was oddly familiar, although I'd never seen her before. She had brown hair and intelligent yellow-green eyes.

When she turned and saw me she looked startled, as if I'd surprised her. "Annalyn?"

"Yes." I reached out to shake her hand as she came over to meet me.

It took her a moment to collect her thoughts. "I'm

Anrita Desai, an old friend of your mother's. She asked me to stop by."

"When did you see her?" I blurted, shocked to realize that this was someone who not only knew my mother but who, by being here, gave me the first indication of her possible interest in me.

"Not long ago. In Los Santos."

"On Earth? I thought she was in deep space."

"She was." She turned my hand over and looked at the palm, then reached for the other hand and studied it. Both had blisters from my work the day before. "Are they treating you all right here?" Her eyes searched mine, as if to judge my honesty.

I explained how I got the blisters and she frowned.

"Are you happy?"

"Yes." I spoke quickly to hide the fact that I resented her question. This stranger couldn't possibly care if I was happy or not. And if she was asking for my mother's sake, my mother couldn't care too much or she wouldn't have left me.

There was an awkward silence until she said, "Your mother asked me to deliver the gift I have waiting outside. Come and see."

I followed her though the lobby and out to the street, where a yellow rental robocar from the spaceport waited by the curb. On the passenger seat was a small robot.

Raising the door, she said, "Hector, disembark." The robot turned about-face and hopped from the seat to the pavement. Whoever designed his locomotion had watched the birds of Earth.

The color of dark wood grain, he looked like a cross between a toy and a utility model. A round body was surmounted by a boxy head from which sprouted antennae. Two lenses and a speaker grill gave the impression of a face. Sturdy legs ended in Y-feet. Arms folded into a holster slot in his middle. Screens and receptors of various colors and textures spotted his body so that he appeared to have polka dots.

"Hector Protector, this is Annalyn Court, your new owner. From now on you will respond only to her voice commands. Prepare to voice imprint as she says her name, followed by the phrase 'twinkle, twinkle, little star.' "

"Ready." Hector's voice was neuter.

As the woman pointed to me I supressed the urge to laugh and said, "Annalyn Court. Twinkle, twinkle, little star."

"Hector, erase the voice imprint command of Anrita Desai," she ordered, followed by, "sit down, Hector."

Hector ignored her.

"Tell him to sit down, Annalyn."

"Sit down, Hector."

To my delight he did so at once by telescoping his leg rods and sinking to the pavement.

"Good," said Anrita. "He's yours." She reached into a pocket and handed me a data caplet. "The owner's manual and warranty."

"How did you reprogram him for me? Can anyone tell him to do that?"

"No. He'll answer only to you now. He was programmed to obey me when I picked him up at the factory." She absentmindedly patted his shoulder, as if he were alive. "Hector Protector is more than a security robot. As you will learn when you have time to get acquainted and study his manual."

"But I don't need protection."

"Not here perhaps. But you may enjoy his company."

"I don't think I can keep him here," I said. "We weren't allowed to bring any games or toys to the academy. I could only bring my guitar."

"Hector is not a toy," she said firmly. "And, I've already secured permission from General Offrey. You can keep Hector in your room."

"Thank you so much for bringing him." I was sure this gift was going to be a burden, but Shala would want me to be polite. Besides, I was hurt that my mother, who couldn't be bothered with me in person, had sent a robot substitute.

Her errand done, Anrita Desai left immediately. I never saw her again or met anyone who knew her.

The odd thing was, it wasn't until a long time later that it occurred to me that my visitor might have been, not my mother's friend, but my mother. I checked the last picture in my mother's file and the face was similar, but not the same. She could have had it redone.

As I had suspected, Sergeant Assam wasn't pleased to see Hector. At first she said I'd have to put it in storage until I graduated. When she reluctantly confirmed my story that the commandant had said I could keep the robot, she was even less happy.

"Favoritism, pure and simple," she grumbled. "Take it up to your room and then get back to the lecture."

She didn't even smile to see Hector start to walk when I said, "Follow me, Hector." But by her age, she'd probably seen a lot of robots.

5

AFTER SHOWING OFF MY EXPENSIVE GIFT TO EVAN and a few other friends, I almost forgot about it. First-year cadets' schedules leave little free time. Hector Protector stood in a corner of my room, ignored, until late one night. I'd just finished studying for a test the next day when a voice said:

"Talk to me!"

It startled me so I jumped and hit my knee on the desk. I was alone, or thought I was. Looking around, suspecting someone was playing a joke on me, my glance fell on Hector.

"Talk to me, Annalyn Court."

"You scared me! I thought you were shut off."

"Protector robots do not shut off," said Hector. "We cannot protect in the OFF mode."

"I suppose not . . ." It had never occurred to me that he might be capable of intelligent conversation—a robot so sophisticated that he got bored? I grinned at him, delighted by the idea, and curious as to what such a robot might want to talk about—so I asked him. "What would you like to talk about?"

"How I may serve you."

"There's nothing I *need* you to do," I decided after

some thought. "Cadets aren't allowed to use artificial intelligence on class work—"

The keyboard message light flashed and I touched it. It was the house computer, advising me my monthly allowance had been credited to my savings account.

"I wish I could spend some of my money," I said, then explained to Hector. "Cadets aren't allowed to go into Midtown and shop. Just visit. Sergeant Assam says that's because most of us are spoiled and need to learn self-discipline. Which includes not buying everything we think we want. But you can't help me with that."

"Clarify," said Hector. "Is the phrase 'you can't help me' an assumption or a rule?"

"An assumption," I admitted.

"For your information, I am equipped with all forms of protection," said Hector. "Including financial. With your permission I will research your financial situation and advise you on the most profitable way to invest your capital. May I utilize your work station?"

"I guess so." I wasn't sure what capital was. What if I didn't want it invested?

"Please access your account." Hector walked over to my study station. When my account record appeared on screen, he inserted the tip of one *finger* into an access portal.

"Your current cash assets total three thousand four hundred and seven credits. That is your capital. We will keep ten percent in savings, in case you do need to purchase anything, and invest the balance."

"In what?" I'd been thinking of investing in a power bike as soon as possible.

"I will analyze all necessary market data and make the proper investments. With your permission," said Hector. When I hesitated, he added, "A Protector robot does nothing to harm its owner. You may trust me."

"What if you lose it?" Three thousand credits seemed like a lot of money to me.

"I will not lose it."

"Can you make me rich?"

"Our initial investment is small. I cannot guarantee so high a level of performance. I can guarantee you will never have less money than you have now."

There was a long silence while I thought it over. "OK."

"Thank you," said Hector.

After I got into bed I lay thinking. "Hector? If you can access things like stock market data, can you also find out about other things? Like mind transfers? I want to know if I have a computer chip buried in my brain."

Hector took a moment to disengage from what he was doing before saying, "Do you need that information immediately?"

"As soon as possible. If you can." I didn't think he could. I had tried and gotten only an encyclopedia entry that referred to mind transplants as "pie-in-the-sky" theory.

Almost a week later Hector made his report to me. He began by saying: "I have failed. Personal medical files are impregnable. I cannot learn if you have had a mind-transfer implant.''

''You mean there are such things?''

''Yes.''

''Who decides who gets them?''

''The Committee.''

''What committee?''

''It had no other name.'' Seeming to sense my disappointment, Hector added, ''I did gain access to secret data on the general topic. Do you wish to hear it all or a summary?''

''A summary.''

''Very well. In the late twentieth century Earth researchers on the initial project wept at the thought that they would be the last generation to die. Their self-pity was premature; a successful MT procedure was not achieved for another century.

''The basic concept is simple: a microscopic monitoring device is surgically implanted in the corpus callosum —the band of neural fibers uniting the two hemispheres of the human brain. The corpus callosum is a massive midline conduit for processing and relaying data—a living communications cable.

''The implant transmits all data passing through that cable to storage outside the body, thus making an exact copy of the mind. When the body's various systems seriously malfunction or cease to function, altering or depriving the brain's nutrients, the MT unit shuts off. Ultimately the living mind is replaced by the copy.''

"The person dies and the copy takes over?" That was what Evan had told me.

"In a sense, yes. The transferred mind can be placed in various protective housings. Contemplatives, for example, might choose simple structures equipped only with visual and vocal links. They usually wish to be placed in scenic locations on Earth. More active types choose mobile forms, such as a robot body.

"The most expensive housing is an android replica of the human at his or her physical peak, often with enhanced appearance and muscular capability.

"The voice is the hardest thing to duplicate. Few people know what their own voice sounds like to others. They do not believe the voice they hear from their copy is truly their own. The new voice is an amalgam of their voice, done by an expert mixer, to achieve the most pleasing sound.

"Mind-transfer research began as an idealistic means of saving great minds for the benefit of all of society. But once in practice, apparently, influence, power, and wealth determined who in fact benefited—the Committee chose politicians, business leaders, entertainment superstars, athletes, and others of that ilk. Actual names were not listed, only the subjects' professions. Truly great minds, you see, are rare and seldom hold positions of wealth and power.

"Early transplants were unstable. For example, the complexity of both vision and the dreaming process was not fully understood; intermittent blindness as well as madness developed during the process and worsened after transfer. Some defective copies were deliberately deleted."

"By whom? And was that considered murder?"

"Deletion was done by research scientists. Ethics are not mentioned."

"Does the MT copy have new dreams, or just reruns?"

"Apparently both. A mind deprived of the ability to dream goes mad," said Hector.

"If you became an android, or a robot, you'd never have to sleep or eat again." The full implications of the idea were hard to imagine at first, but the more obvious did occur to me. "You could go anywhere outside without a pressure suit. Keep your money forever and always get richer, because you'd never die. You'd remember everything forever . . ."

"All that is correct, if crudely reasoned," agreed Hector. "To totally destroy an MT mind, all its copies must be found and deleted. This is apparently difficult, since copies are hidden in a variety of places, for optimum security. The penalty for unlawfully destroying or attempting to delete an MT unit is death for mortals, total deletion for an MT."

"How do you delete them?"

"The easiest way would be to implant a virus and cause an MT unit to erase itself and all copies," said Hector. "I do not know if that is the official form of execution."

"Who could do that? And how?"

"The Committee. I do not know how they would gain access to the system."

"What if I had an MT chip in my brain and wanted it taken out?" I asked.

"I found no data on that subject."

"If a person dies, and only his or her mind is in what is a machine—are they the machine? Do they have a soul?"

"Legal and metaphysical questions are not discussed in the research data," said Hector. "Are you asking if the copy is unique, as humans perceive themselves to be unique?"

"No. I mean, if you believe people have a soul or spirit, and that soul leaves intact when the body dies, does the mind know it's gone? Do other people know? Does the copy seem like the same person they knew?"

"Souls and spirits were not discussed," said Hector. "Do I have your permission to return to your finances?"

"Just one more question. Are you an MT, Hector? Were you alive once?"

Hector didn't answer for twenty seconds, a very long time for a computer of his high caliber. "I do not know," he said. "If I knew, I would be restricted from admitting it."

6

TIME AT THE ACADEMY PASSED QUICKLY. OUR EDucation was almost too thorough. In addition to military subjects, sciences, and the classics, we studied logic and economics and had endless computer courses. The latter were necessary so that we future officers might knowledgeably supervise the technicians who, I slowly came to understand, truly controlled life on Mars.

My favorite courses involved learning to drive or fly all sorts of vehicles, and learning to repair them. I discovered I liked working with my hands. It was fun trying to figure out what was wrong with an aircar; being able to repair it gave me a real sense of satisfaction.

The worst courses, so far as I was concerned, were about internal security. For the first time, I learned my father was repeatedly the target of assassination attempts. The very idea shocked me.

"Why?" I asked Sergeant Assam, who was one of the Security instructors. "I don't believe that. Who would want to kill him?"

The sergeant fixed me with a noncommital stare, then with her right forefinger she slowly traced the line of the scar down the side of her face and said, "I assure you it's the truth, Cadet Court. This scar will testify to my defense of the President in one such attempt."

"But who would do such a thing?"

"Their names don't matter," she said. "All of them die for their crime. But I can tell you they include elites as well as commoners. Some resent the power the President commands. Others want to take power for themselves. A few are simply insane—flawed minds that escaped detection.

"The need to protect the President at all times is the main reason behind our law that says that in his presence everyone must assume the Attitude of Respect. When you are on your knees, with your fingers locked behind your neck and your head bowed, it's hard to draw a weapon without attracting a guard's attention."

Sergeant Assam gave us a wry smile. "In whatever way you may serve the President, you are also responsible for his security. At all times. His security is your prime purpose."

Listening to her, thinking how she'd gotten that scar, my respect for her bravery increased in direct proportion to my understanding that, like her, all of us could risk death protecting the President . . . who Evan said was an android. He had to have been joking; nobody would die for an android.

Evan loved those Security courses as much as I hated them. He still wasn't a good student academically, although academy discipline and Sergeant Assam kept him in line, but he enjoyed and excelled in marksmanship and martial arts.

When we were paired in assassin drills, I could target him only if I could make him lose his temper. All our training weapons shot or exploded marker dyes to indicate hits. He "killed" me with dye spots at least once a week.

I found the most difficult assassination attempts to spot were the bombs. Evan seemed able to sense where they would be hidden. "Just think where you'd put a bomb," he'd say. But try as I might, I spent a lot of time in that course, too, scrubbing off dye. Evan was almost never hit.

As a third-year cadet I went outside the shields for the first time in my life. To walk and work on the real surface of the planet, I wore an insulated pressure suit with its own heat and air supply . . . knowing that without it my blood would boil before I could take a breath and start to freeze before my body hit the ground. I was terrified.

Learning to wear a pressure suit was the hardest part of my education. Just putting one on still bothers me. I hate the taut feel of being encased like a sausage, hate looking out through the helmet. Being isolated from smell and touch makes me feel unreal.

Cadets who couldn't tolerate pressure suits were potential problems in emergencies and could be expelled from the academy. For that reason I kept my fears to myself, thinking no one else would ever guess.

That went on for weeks until one afternoon when I came back from a surface exercise and Sergeant Assam met me at the airlock.

"Congratulations," she said, looking pleased. "Your pulse remained almost normal the entire time out."

"What does that mean?"

"All suits contain vital signs monitors. It takes courage to be as frightened as you've been and still go out there. But you worked through the fear."

"You *knew* I was scared?"

"Only fools aren't afraid of the surface."

We had extensive training in courtesy and protocol, so we learned the complex social system of official life. Some cadets served as pages at major social functions in Fountain House, from dinner parties to the rare funeral. To be named a page was a great honor, for it meant one ranked among the top ten cadets at the academy.

From the beginning I studied hard and did my best to achieve top ranking. I wanted to be a page. Not for the honor, but because I thought it would give me a chance to meet my father.

When I told Evan my plans, he laughed and said, "Why do you care so much about him, Annie? It's plain he doesn't care about you. Besides, you shouldn't attract his attention."

"Why not?"

"He doesn't want to see you, Mother says. Because he hates your mother. He's never forgiven her for leaving."

"He told Janis that?"

"Well . . . she says everybody knows it."

What I didn't tell him was what had become my main reason for wanting to meet the President: I was afraid

Evan hadn't been joking that night on the Green, afraid my father *was* an android.

I became a page in the middle of my senior year.

Several days later Evan was also made a page, by special presidential appointment. Since he was not a good student, rumors—and resentment—quickly spread. I thought it was unfair, but I didn't blame him. He couldn't help it if his mother had obviously pulled strings.

MY FIRST TIME EVER IN THE PRESIDENTIAL WING
of Fountain House was as a page at the President's annual
Founders' Day dinner to pay tribute to the pioneers who
settled Mars.

The place was dazzling; the Sanctuary was luxurious,
but nothing like these official state rooms. I found myself
wishing that everyone on Mars could see this beauty—
Security forbade all filming in this part of the building.

The enormous rooms were sumptuous beyond imagi-
nation—richly furnished, deeply carpeted, gleaming with
crystal and gold. The party was in the Emerald Ballroom,
called that because one back-lighted wall was paneled
with mosaics of emerald crystal. Banks of flowers rimmed
the dance floor; hidden lighted fountains sprayed misty
rainbows. The guests looked like flowers, too, all dressed
in pastels.

For me, the important moment came when a three-
note bell tone sounded, signaling the President's approach. The music died. The guests stopped dancing and
faced the balcony on the emerald wall. At a fourth bell
all knelt, hands clasped behind necks, heads bowed, silent
in the Attitude of Respect.

At the rear of the balcony a panel slid back to reveal

a gleaming wood-paneled hallway. Four armed guards in formal dress filed out and surveyed the ballroom. They carried golden guns. You could have heard the proverbial pin drop by the time they stepped aside and the President appeared, flanked by several dignitaries.

Seeing him made me lose all discretion. Instead of focusing on the floor, I stared up at him and slowly broke into a smile of pleasure and relief. Because there he was, *in person*, not on a screen. And he looked exactly as a person should if he or she ruled the world. I felt such pride that he was *my* father. No android could project his confident sense of power. He had to be the real thing.

Tall and handsome, with golden skin, his black hair was streaked with silver. He wore a white uniform, a short cape lined with green, and his belt and high collar were stiff with pavé diamonds. Cradled in his right arm he carried his staff of office, a platinum baton topped by an emerald ball. True or not, every cadet in the academy *knew* the baton was really a deadly lal gun.

As he gazed around the room, from right to left and back again, his glance fell on me and held. Noting where he was looking, a guard saw me and raised her weapon, but he said something and the gun was lowered.

For what seemed a long time but was no more than seconds we studied each other's faces. Then, to my great joy and terror, he beckoned me to approach. I managed to stand with my hands still clasped behind my neck, weave my way among the kneeling guests, and climb the steps to the balcony.

He watched me all the way. Even when we were almost face-to-face, he didn't speak but just kept looking. I felt my face flush. His skin was flawless, his eyelashes longer than mine, his eyes so black they looked almost liquid. It was easy to understand why women found him so irresistible.

In the silence clothes rustled as some of the kneeling guests shifted in discomfort—or curiosity. This attention being paid to me would be a topic of conversation for days.

When he finally spoke, his whisper was soft and he smiled for the benefit of the audience, but he sounded very stern.

"Who do you think you are to disobey the rules?"

"I'm your daughter, sir."

Visibly startled, he turned to his protocol officer, who leaned closer to him and murmured something. He froze, then slowly smiled again. At *me*. "You're Annalyn Court?"

"Yes, sir." My heart was pounding from a mixture of excitement and fear.

The smile broadened. "How old are you?"

"Sixteen, sir."

"Yes . . ." He nodded to himself. "We must get acquainted. Why don't you sit with me at dinner? Sanders, take care of it," he ordered the protocol aide.

"I'm very honored, sir."

"You should be." He gave me a boyish grin. "Pages never sit with the President. At most, they get to stand behind my chair, like uniformed decorations. But when I saw you down there, smiling up at me . . . I had to know who could look so genuinely happy to see me. I find your daring and honesty refreshing."

And with that he took me by the hand and turned his attention to his other guests. "Thank you all for joining me here tonight to remember and pay tribute once again to the brave men and women whose brilliance and great sacrifice made all this possible. Please rise and join me in singing our national anthem."

The ballroom came alive again as people got to their feet. Some had to help others up. Wrists and knees were being rubbed discretely as trumpets blared the introduction. Raggedly, two hundred voices began to sing the familiar melody.

"Out of the cold came warmth and life,

"Out of wind and darkness, love . . ."

He took me with him to the receiving line and introduced me to his guests. I was so charmed and awed by his attention it was hard to think clearly. Wanting to make him proud of me, I was on my best behavior.

Many of the guests were so famous that I recognized them. To my surprise, all of them greeted me with the same respect they showed the President.

I met my first Terrans that night. It sounds bigoted, but I found them rather repulsive. Compared to the average Martian, the gravity of Earth makes her people seem like giants. They are so tall and strong. Even their hair looks muscular.

When the receiving line had almost ended, an aide escorted me to the head table. I knew Janis would be there but was surprised to see Evan with her. Both were deep in conversation with an off-Mars guest, a pretty girl named Alexa Tyrell, who I'd met in the receiving line.

Also at that table were Council members and diplomats, as well as some of the owners and chief executive officers of Mars's major customers for the crystals and various exquisitely tiny motors we exported. Alexa's family represented one of the biggest customers.

In spite of what the President had said about sitting with him, my seat was across the table, and three chairs down. But I didn't mind; it was a good place from which to watch him.

As I became calmer and could think more clearly, I began to see that although he didn't act like an android, he did look *too perfect*—especially compared to most of the off-world guests, who had natural flaws. But then compared to them, all our Council members looked too perfect.

It did occur to me that the Council members might be androids, but that seemed too far-fetched. I told myself it was logical for them to look good. After all, Mars had the best cell replacement therapy and rejuv technology available—and any elite could afford it.

I must admit that in spite of my excitement at meeting the President, the dinner itself was boring. The conversation was entirely devoted to business or polite chatting. Evan's attention was focused on Alexa, who seemed to find him fascinating. They sat too far away for me to eavesdrop, although I tried.

Compared to the tailored simplicity of our white uniforms, Alexa gleamed in iridescent pink tights under a gauzy pink tunic flecked with gold. Gold arm bracelets clotted with rubies snaked down to her wrists. Gold and ruby earrings swept her shoulders. She wore at least one ruby ring on every finger. Her long, dark hair was loosely secured by more gold.

Looking at her I realized that I had never worn clothes like that—or even thought of doing so. Just uniforms and plain, comfortable sports clothes. And my hair was so short that if I wrapped gold wire around my head like that, people would think I was wearing an antenna.

I didn't see Janis leave her chair, but suddenly she was leaning over me, smelling of perfume and wine. "Isn't it nice they get along so well?" Her face was so close her whisper tickled my ear. "We signed the nuptial contract nearly five years ago, but this is the first time they've met. I'm sure you're as happy for him as I am."

Nuptial contract? Evan had never mentioned that. And this was the person he was going to marry? Evan and this exotic, overdressed alien? How could he?

My expression must have pleased Janis. "But that's right!" she purred with malice. "You didn't know. Alexa," she called across the table, "you and Annalyn must become friends. You have so much in common."

Their conversation interrupted, Evan and Alexa glanced our way. Alexa's smile as she said "Hello, Annalyn" was as polite as it was disinterested, so it was probably just as well Janis gave me no chance to reply before resuming her monologue.

"Alexa's family is one of the Union's most successful," she went on, "and one of Mars's oldest customers.

Not only do the Tyrells own the new Wild Star habitats, but their real estate group controls much of Earth's South American continent and a large part of Antarctica."

"That's very impressive," I said, and meant it.

"Isn't it?" agreed Janis. "Perhaps I shouldn't say this, but it is a shame no one has bothered to arrange a good marriage for you—or any marriage, for that matter." She gave me a pitying smile.

"I never thought about marrying," I said, sounding childish even to myself.

At that Alexa looked from me to Janis with a quick, cold glint in her eyes that suggested she was less than fond of her future mother-in-law. So we did have something in common.

Janis, too, must have caught that glance because she abruptly waved at another guest and called, "Carley, how good to see you!" and was gone.

Evan and Alexa turned away with apologetic smiles and resumed their conversation. I took a sip of water and thought how much I loathed Janis for trying to spoil my evening.

Before the party was over, the Tyrells had to leave to catch their flight. Evan *and* Janis went along to the space-port to see them off. When the chief of pages excused me several hours later, I went back to my room alone, feeling like Cinderella after the ball. I'd no sooner gotten in than Evan was at my door.

"Want to get a sandwich? I'm starved. Alexa talked so much I couldn't eat without looking rude."

"Will you miss her?"

He laughed. "I don't even like her."

"But you're going to marry her?"

"Sure. Six years from now. But it's only a corporate marriage, Annie." He made it sound so casual, so acceptable. "It won't mean anything. Except her company gets favored trade status because I'm the President's son, and I get a lot of money. After the wedding trip, she'll go back to Earth or wherever, and I'll go where I want to."

"Will you have children?"

"One at least," he said easily. "Otherwise our contract is void after seven years and my settlement is revoked. Alexa can keep the kid if she wants. Or probably Mother will. She'd like that—another little kid to control."

"That's disgusting, Evan."

"What? My mother? She—"

"Not that. You're marrying Alexa just for money?"

He'd been staring out the window, and when he turned to me he looked angry. "I need the money, Annie. Mother said I would, and she's right. Our father doesn't give his kids the kind of money I'll need for the position I want."

"That Janis wants, you mean."

"You're not stupid, Annie. You're refusing to understand."

I watched him walk out of my room, heard his door close and lock.

In the quiet the pipes whispered in the walls. Somewhere down the hall a door opened and a raucous burst of music and laughter escaped from a Friday night party.

I wished I was at that party, that I was anywhere else, and anyone but myself. I sat down at my desk and began to cry.

"Question." As usual Hector's unexpected voice made me jump. "Are you crying?"

"Yes."

"Why?"

"Because I'm not happy . . . But don't worry about it."

"I am your protector. I must worry about you."

Perhaps because I felt so miserable, I wanted to hug him. Instead I picked up a sock from the floor and dusted his head, then wiped away tears that had fallen on him.

"You can worry about my finances," I said. "You never have told me how much I'm worth."

"You wish to know your total assets?"

"Yes, please."

"In approximately forty-six hours, when several stock exchanges open, I can give you an exact figure, but as of three days ago your total worth was one hundred ninety-three thousand, seven hundred and eighty-one credits."

"What?"

Interpreting my amazement as lack of comprehension, Hector repeated the figure and added, "The total would have been greater, but a bond investment vaporized when a stray meteoroid struck a habitat still under construction."

"You've made me rich! You're wonderful!" And then I did hug him—and bruised myself.

"I am a Protector robot," said Hector, oblivious to my emotion. "You are not rich. You are millions of credits from that state."

But in spite of what Hector thought, to me it seemed like a fortune. And the best thing was, now I could grant Shala's wish and get her the café she'd always wanted.

And I did. With Hector's help, I went into Midtown to look at property—and bought a café and leased the land beneath it. To keep her from feeling indebted, we made Shala the managing partner. Within months of opening, she told me proudly that Shala's Place was the most popular nightspot in Midtown. The monthly figures soon proved she was as good at making money as Hector.

Whenever I could get away from the academy, I'd hurry and change and go in to Shala's Place for dinner and the music. The Midtowners who came there all seemed nice, relaxed, and informal. They also seemed to feel any friend of Shala's was a friend of theirs. After I got over being shy, I even took my guitar along and joined in sometimes, when the other musicians weren't too professional.

8

I KNOW IT WAS NAIVE, BUT I WAS SURPRISED AND depressed by the way my life changed because the President noticed me.

By the next day officers and instructors were treating me with deference. All except Sergeant Assam. She was as demanding as ever, which made me respect her even more. Cadets I barely knew acted like old friends. And a few people I thought were my friends began avoiding me.

Total strangers sent flowers; merchants sent gifts, which I returned. And all because they thought I had influence with the President.

A few days later, without warning, George Burgess, the President's oldest son and official heir, paid an unexpected visit to the academy. An alumnus, he was now a general. A full-dress review was held in his honor.

Evan and I were leaving the parade field when an officer met us and said we were to report to the commandant's office at once. General Burgess was there when we arrived. Several of his aides stood stiffly flanking the door. General Offrey greeted us casually and invited us to sit. General Burgess frowned in disapproval.

Rejuvenation makes it impossible to guess anyone's

real age, but George Burgess's good looks were remarkable even in a world obsessed by physical perfection.

After looking the two of us over as if he were going to buy us, he said, "So. You're supposedly my half-brother and half-sister?"

"Yes, sir." Evan answered for both of us.

"You're younger than some of my grandchildren."

I didn't risk a glance at Evan to see if that bit of information shocked him. If the President's oldest son could have grandchildren, *how old* was the President?

"How many children do you have, sir?" Evan asked —in an effort to make polite conversation, I thought.

Burgess gave him a disdainful look from his glittering green eyes. "Not nearly so many as my esteemed father." An offending smudge on his left ring finger preoccupied him for a moment. His long, narrow hands looked much older than the rest of him. "Three," he said, eyeing Evan again. "And eight grandchildren. You will inherit almost nothing."

There was no logical reason to fear him, but my heart began beating too fast. I was glad General Offrey was there.

"My mother, Lani Burgess, was his first wife," Burgess went on. "His only *real* wife. My late brother and I are his only true sons. My children and grandchildren are his only true heirs. And, incidentally, while one of my grandchildren is a cadet, she isn't a member of the Page Corps."

"Unfortunately, her academic qualifications—"

"Stay out of this!" General Burgess ordered the commandant in a tone that would have silenced even Janis. "I'm not talking to you. I'm explaining things to these two. I want them to know I will outlive them both—no matter what they may have been told. As will my children and grandchildren."

With that he gave us a too-sweet smile and abruptly rose, saying, "Enjoy your natural lifetimes—while you can."

The interview was ended.

"Are you threatening—"

But General Burgess was gone before the commandant could finish the sentence, the aides practically tripping over one another trying to follow their master out.

"I'm not sure what that was all about," General Offrey admitted as his office door hissed shut, "but I will advise the President of his son's remarks. However, until further notice, stay inside the academy grounds. Don't eat or drink anything that isn't shared by us all, and go nowhere alone. Those are orders."

It was clear General Offrey thought George Burgess had threatened to kill us, while I thought the general had told us that he and his family had MT implants—but Evan and I didn't. Which, if it was true, was a relief. But that phrase "while you can" also bothered me.

"Sir, may I have permission to speak with my mother?" Evan asked. "Right away?"

"Granted. Then return to your regular class."

I considered calling Shala, but decided not to. If I was in danger, there was no way she could protect me, so why scare her and worry her sick for nothing? Instead, I talked to Hector that night.

"I interpret George Burgess's remarks to mean," said Hector, "that he wants to intimidate by making you fear him; he wants you to believe that either you have no MT implant or, if you do, that he can destroy your copy. You may disregard his remark concerning inheritances. George Burgess would have no control over the President's will."

"Do you think he would try to kill us?" I asked, shaken.

"No," said Hector. "He threatened you in front of witnesses. And if he could destroy your mind-transfer copies, why threaten? Why not do it? Thus I conclude he wants you to think he has power over you"—Hector paused—"or soon will."

"How could he?"

"I lack the necessary data to answer that."

Evan never told me what he and Janis discussed, and I was too proud to ask. Ever since the night of the Founders' Day dinner there had been a wall between us. That depressed me, and I missed him as much as if he'd gone away.

Several weeks later the news network announced that General Burgess had been appointed military liasion to the Martian Federation of Manufacturing States and would be permanently stationed in their new headquarters on Phobos.

When we heard the news I told Evan, "He's too far away now to kill us. We can relax."

Evan disagreed. "Old George wouldn't kill us himself. He'd hire someone. Mother says there are lots of people who'd kill anyone for five hundred credits."

"Janis likes being dramatic," I scoffed. "Who would be stupid enough to risk the death penalty for so little money?"

"Evan's mother is right," Hector said when I told him later.

"But why?" I asked. "Risk death by exposure for only five hundred credits? No one is that poor on Mars."

"Not true," said Hector.

"It is! We learned that in primary school."

"That data is incorrect," Hector insisted. "You will locate the error if you review human history here.

"As you know, Mars was settled by technocrats— well-paid, highly trained corporate employees from Earth. Most were induced to come here on false pretenses. Their contracts called for a six-year stay. Few would have come for any amount had they known how the construction crews suffered during the four years it took to build the living and factory quarters."

"I thought robots did the construction," I said.

"Only the cruder work. Robotic technology of that era was much less advanced than today's. As I was saying, after the stress of a two-year flight to Mars, the technocrats arrived to find their new underground quarters were similar to and as cramped as the spaceship they'd just vacated. Outside was a completely barren surface, twilight, inhuman cold, and endless sandstorms. Home-Earth was six-years-plus-a-two-year-trip away. Drugs could not control their deep, clinical depression. Tempers flared. There were murders.

"Within a year, more than half were sterile. By the time they made adequate living and factory space and had built the defense system to protect their technology, infertility had risen to eighty percent. Pregnancies ended in miscarriage. Of the few live births, only fifty-two percent survived their first year.

"As a result, many people died without heirs, leaving their property to friends. Each generation saw wealth become more concentrated among a small group of people."

"If it was so horrible here, why didn't they all just leave?" I asked. "Go back to Earth?"

"Many did, but because of the enormous salaries and benefits offered by the developing consortium, there were always more than enough replacements. In time, humans adapted, the colony became self-sufficient, the technology extremely profitable.

"The colonists then asked for and got a larger share of the profits by threatening to wage a war of rebellion, which the consortium had no hope of winning—because of the very defense system it had designed to protect its huge investment. Eventually the colonists negotiated complete independence.

"After independence was declared, it was a simple matter for those who had become rich on Mars to slant the new charter's laws in their favor, to make their good fortune ongoing—"

"Were there MT's back then?" I interrupted him to ask.

"It is probable," said Hector, "but impossible to check. By the time the domed surface towns were complete, eliminating radiation and atmospheric problems, almost all of the now immensely valuable land beneath the domes was purchased by the rich. The common tech, on salary, could not afford to buy it.

"When people began to immigrate to Mars, the landowners refused to sell; they would only lease. From real estate profits alone they quickly went from being rich technocrats to an immensely wealthy and powerful elite.

"Since independence, those who cooperate with the elite ruling class are well treated. Those few who openly question the status quo often die or are assigned to a ship headed for deep space. Since most common citizens on Mars are technicians or researchers, any question of their loyalty means their careers are ruined, and they are denied permission to travel or emigrate on grounds of national security. Mars exists on technology, most of it top secret, all of it highly marketable.

"In short, Annalyn, it is highly probable that among the common class there are some who might kill an elite for free—to say nothing of five hundred credits—and feel a sense of justice as well as satisfaction in doing so."

At first I didn't believe Hector. I knew the President was in danger from assassins, but it had never occurred to me that I might be too. Still . . . why was it called the Sanctuary? And why had Janis always been so worried about kidnappers?

I did some research on my own. Afterward Hector went with me whenever I left the academy grounds.

THE WILD RUMORS BEGAN SOON: OF PEOPLE PLOT-
ting to overthrow the government, of plans to kill the
President, of espionage. Or maybe I just began to listen
to them because of Hector's history lesson.

One disturbing rumor said armed strangers had been
arrested in The Fountains complex. No one knew how
they got in, or what happened to them afterward.

I didn't believe it. The Fountains was the most heav-
ily secured area on Mars. You'd need a secret tunnel to
enter or leave undetected.

Within days there was a rumor of an old secret
tunnel being found. Before sealing it, people whispered,
Security traced wheel prints in the dust all the way back
to the spaceport. Again, no one could provide exact
details.

Then, during one of the President's rare public ap-
pearances at an award ceremony in Midtown, some of
the audience had to be stunned into the Attitude of Respect. The crowd turned ugly, and the President was
rushed to the safety of his car.

Both Evan and I were members of the President's
honor guard by this time, and Evan was on duty that day.

There was nothing about the incident on the news, but Evan told me what happened.

"I didn't expect it," he said, clearly shaken. "The crowd always obeys. But this time they didn't—I got the feeling that if they wanted to get him, they'd kill us to do it. And we couldn't stop them. Next time you're on duty, be careful."

"Was the President scared?"

"No. He had them all arrested for treason."

"The people who wouldn't kneel?"

"The whole crowd. To set an example."

"That's not fair."

Evan shrugged. "The President called it 'a psychological deterrent.' "

If there was a trial we didn't hear about it at the academy. And the honor guard wasn't put on special alert, despite new rumors of death threats against the President and several Council members.

Then I heard that many of the ambassadors were leaving Mars. It was said they'd been recalled and replacements would be arriving soon, but all the embassy staffs left, too.

For the first time, there were vacant buildings on Embassy Row. Yet there had been no announcements, no farewell parties. Officially, it hadn't happened. That was when I started to worry.

Despite his skill in tapping the computer networks, Hector couldn't confirm the rumors. He did assure me, though, that "Martian stocks show no weakness," which he interpreted as a sign of the government's stability.

One morning I was wakened by the arrival of one of the President's aides at my door. She handed me sealed orders and left without a word. Still half-asleep, I slit the seal.

Effective immediately, the order said, I was promoted to the rank of commander and given a temporary assignment on the sweeper ship *Capri*. I had four hours to catch the military shuttle out to the ship, where I would receive further orders. The commandant had been advised of my assignment.

The orders bore the President's handwritten signature and were time-dated ten hours before. Which was odd; supposedly he was away on a trip. I assumed he returned the night before.

I was still dazedly rereading the orders when my door rang again and three new uniforms were delivered, each bearing a commander's gold stars.

Not knowing if I should feel honored at being jumped two grades in rank before graduation, or scared to death at being sent into space, I was both. But mostly, I was bewildered.

Why me? Why not Evan? He wanted to go to space. I didn't. All I could think of was Hector telling me about people who suddenly found themselves on a ship bound for deep space. But I'd done nothing wrong.

I wanted to talk to Evan, but he'd already gone up to breakfast. I dressed in street clothes and caught the train into Midtown to tell Shala good-bye.

"I'm very worried," she told me over breakfast. She spoke in a near whisper, although we were alone in her apartment over the café. "People in Midtown are angry. People have disappeared since the President was here the last time. You can't find out what happened to them, and Security just pretends to help. One of my best singers is missing. They say it's happened before and it has to stop. That the elite have everything and commoners have no say. That Mars was supposed to be a democracy."

She looked at me, her eyes dark with concern. "I think some people are planning . . ."

"You're not part of this 'they,' are you, Shala?" I asked, thoroughly worried. "Please, I don't know what's happening, but I don't want you to disappear."

She shook her head. "No. I try not to listen. I don't want to know. But I'm worried. And I don't like it that you are going away."

Time was short, and when I had to go, she burst into tears and hugged me tightly.

When I got back to the academy, Evan's door was open. He was in his room, packing. Seeing that he was also wearing a commander's stars made me feel better. I said the first thing I thought: "Are you assigned to the *Capri*, too?"

He jumped as if I'd shot him. "Hey, learn to knock! You scared the—" Seeing my uniform made him pause. "You, too? Congratulations, Commander. What's the *Capri*?"

Disappointment swept over me. "Where are you going?"

"Itek." That was a small city to the northeast. "Secret orders." He went back to his packing.

"Do you know what's happening, Evan?" I was going to tell him what Shala said, then decided not to; he might tell Janis. "Why are we being sent away on special assignments so close to graduation? Is there an emergency?"

"I think it's a final test, to see how we react," he said. "Don't worry. We'll be fine. So what's the *Capri*?"

"I'm almost ashamed to tell you. It's a sweeper ship."

"A garbage cruiser?" He laughed. "In that fancy uniform?"

"Is your assignment more glamorous? You're a commander, too," I said. "And you're the one who's always wanted to go into space."

He frowned as if something had just occurred to him, then motioned for me to shut the door. When I had, he turned on the white noise for added security. "Annie, did you hear any rumors about a ship being lost between here and Phobos?"

"No. What about it?"

"Supposedly it was blown up. They say a rebel faction took over Phobos—led by the moon's governor. And he and the ringleaders were coming here to present formal demands to the President and Council when their ship disappeared on-screen."

"But Phobos is our moon. Their ships are protected by our defense system. If it's true, either the defense system misfired . . . or the ship was deliberately destroyed."

I shivered in spite of myself, wondering which sector the *Capri* was in. "When did this happen?"

He shook his head. "I don't know. I . . . maybe last night? Maybe that's what your orders are about. Cleaning up the wreck."

"Janis told you about the ship?"

"It's just a rumor," he repeated, but I knew that wasn't true. A rumor like that would have spread over the academy in minutes, been common gossip in Midtown in an hour. I would have heard it from one of the cadets or from Shala. What Evan was telling me was top secret information. Our assignments weren't "a test."

"Does this 'rumor' have anything to do with your going to Itek?"

"I don't think so," he said, but he had that embarrassed expression he always got when his mother had wangled some privilege for him.

I decided Janis must have asked for him to be sent away from the city to keep him safe. And maybe that's why I was being sent away. But by whom—my father? And safe from what? Did this mean all the rumors were true? Including what Shala had said? That would explain why the ambassadors had left so quickly.

"Is Olympia in danger?"

"No!"

"Is the President staying here? Is your mother?"

"He isn't back yet. Now no more questions. I can't tell you anything more without getting us both into trouble."

"How much should I worry?"

"Annie, don't get dramatic. Just follow orders," he said. "You're lucky. You get to go to space. I don't. But I have to go soon and I'm not finished packing."

Before I could take the hint the door chimed and we both jumped.

"The baggage drone is here," Hector said when I opened the door. "If I am to go with the drone, you must affix this seal to my arm." He handed me a hooked seal.

"I don't know if you can go." I'd forgotten about him and immediately felt guilty.

"How can I protect you if I'm not with you?"

"Take it along," Evan said impatiently.

"But what if they won't let him onboard? I don't want to leave him at the dock. He might be stolen. Or damaged."

"Wait." Turning to his terminal Evan typed instead of using voice command. There was no way for me to see who he contacted and I knew better than to ask. As Janis's son he had influence and ways of accomplishing things. "Commander Court's protector robot will go with her" he typed. "Confirm."

After some delay the words appeared onscreen: "Confirmed. Her robot has been cleared for transfer to the *Capri.*"

"My pleasure," he said lightly when I tried to thank him. Something in his tone made me feel I was already in his past, already gone. "Go on, Annie. I'm not through packing. Send the drone back for my bag. Oh, and enjoy your trip."

Catching my hand he gave it a quick farewell squeeze. To soften any impression that he was hurrying me off, he grinned down at the robot, saying, "Hector, take good care of her."

Hector, programmed to obey me only, ignored him.

10

MARS HAS FOUR SWEEPER SHIPS LIKE THE *CAPRI*, all ugly. They look like crabs and bristle with antennae. The command deck and crew quarters are in the front. Bulging viewports suggest eyes. The ships move slowly through space, clawlike arms extended, trapping orbiting debris and feeding it, via sorter arms, into yawning bins in the belly.

Preoccupied by my own thoughts, I missed the *Capri*'s approach. By the time the shuttle docked with the sweeper, all I could see were orange and yellow lights flashing in the darkness outside the viewport.

Airlocks sealed. The floor hatch beeped a warning, hissed sharply, and lifted. With the air exchange between vessels, a cold, metallic odor flowed into the shuttle cabin. One whiff and a wave of nausea swept over me, the result of fear as much as the lack of gravity.

The shuttle steward hooked the grabline to the wall ring by my recliner. "Take your time," she said as I fumbled with the release on my restraining nets. "There's no hurry." Either she guessed this was my first real gravity-free flight, or she was routinely kind.

As I floated along the grabline three other shuttle passengers, two men and a woman, prepared to disembark.

They wore the ominous black uniforms of the secret service. Collar insignia identified them as sergeants. Self-absorbed, I hadn't noticed them before; obviously they were going to be my staff on this assignment. I should have introduced myself, acknowledged them. Now they probably thought I was just another arrogant elite brat in an officer's uniform.

I was still a few feet from the hatch, trying to figure out how to enter it without bumping into the steward, when a sergeant pushed away from her seat. With practiced ease she torpedoed past me, did a graceful somersault off the forward bulkhead and dropped feet first down the boarding tube.

Impressed, and embarrassed by my own awkwardness, I glanced back to see if the other two were coming, ready to let them pass. They waved me on, their expressions saying they were being polite only because of my rank.

I went down headfirst, using the ladderlike handgrips. I'd no sooner righted myself on the *Capri*'s deck when the SS men landed beside me like ballet dancers and bounded over to stand with their companion. Their name tags read: KIM, RUIZ, and BURKART.

"Commander Court?" A man about ten years my senior greeted me. At the mention of my name, the SS trio exchanged surprised glances and then saluted. As I acknowledged them, Hector was lowered through the hatch, followed by our personal gear and four pressure suits.

"I'm Saji Utman, captain of the *Capri*. Let me help

you with these." Without waiting for a reply he knelt, grabbed one of my feet and slipped a mag-loc over my boot. "Now the other foot."

Ignoring my embarrassment at being treated like the novice I was, he stood up, saying, "As soon as we're free of the shuttle and can accelerate, we'll go back on artgrav. Then you'll feel more normal. In the meantime, there's my office. You can listen to your orders in privacy. I'll take your gear to your cabin, show your people their bunks, and come back for instructions."

The President himself had recorded my orders. Listening to him, I hardly noticed when the shuttle, my last link with home, had gone and gravity returned.

As Evan had guessed, I was to supervise the recovery of the still-orbiting wreckage of a military ship. I made a note of the coordinates where the wreck was located.

I was to check all bodies for data capsules. The bodies were then to be placed in containers that were already aboard the *Capri*. Equipment debris was to be kept separate and hand searched by the secret service. If they found any floating data capsules, they were to give them to me.

"Under no circumstances will any of you listen to these capsules. You will hand deliver all of them to me and to me only." He repeated "to me only" twice.

Once collected, the wreckage would be off-loaded onto shuttles that, at my signal, would be dispatched to meet the *Capri*. He gave me a code number and phrase to use in signaling him that the shuttles should be sent.

"Captain Utman," the President's voice continued,

"knows only that his ship is to pick up top secret material. He has been warned that under no condition is he or any of his crew allowed access to any part of this wreckage.

"You were chosen for this mission, Annalyn, because I cannot go myself. I know you will see to it that all is done exactly as I wish. I have complete trust in you."

That was flattering, but why me? He hardly knew me. Why not Evan?

So far as that went, he had other children—at least five of them were experienced military officers. Did he think I was the most trustworthy? Or the most expendable?

A good soldier doesn't question. A good soldier obeys. If my father truly had this much confidence in me, I would do my best to justify his trust.

To be sure I understood, I listened to his orders twice, then pocketed them. The assignment reminded me of my first day at the academy; this was another cleanup job.

Captain Utman was waiting outside. After giving the ship's computer the wreck coordinates, he showed me my quarters.

The *Capri* wasn't designed to carry passengers. The second officer had been relegated to sleeping in the control room. I had his cabin, a compartment so small that when we were both inside, Hector had to stand against the wall, under the vu-screen. The space contained a sleeping sling, locker, and tiny sanit module.

At that I was lucky; the SS sergeants were given sleeping slings in storage spaces. In spite of that, when they met me in the dining room, they were on their best behavior, as if learning who I was had somehow made a difference. Fear?

Kim apologized for them, saying, "We hope you weren't offended by our acrobatics when we left the shuttle. It's hard to resist the chance to play in weightlessness."

"I admired your skill," I said, and then I apologized for my seeming rudeness on the shuttle. The academy had taught us that officers never explained or apologized for their actions, that to do so lessened staff respect. I decided that was bad advice; respect should be mutual.

To change the subject then, I told them as much as they had to know about the assignment.

"You'll have to do body searches, Commander?" Ruiz looked sympathetic.

"Yes." For a commoner to touch an elite, living or dead, was a criminal offense.

To pass the time, and because I like knowing how things work, I asked Captain Utman to tell me all about his ship. At first he thought I was just trying to be polite, but once sure of my interest, he not only gave me an education on sweeper ships, but he also became much more friendly.

The early centuries of Earth's space exploration, he explained, left tons of debris orbiting our solar system at a speed of more than 25,000 miles per hour. Everything from paint chips to rocket boosters, satellites, labs, cameras, tools that escaped the mitted hands of early "astronauts"—and frozen waste from their shuttle toilet dumps. Collision with any of this litter, even a paint chip,

can be deadly. The sweeper ship was designed to remove
these dangers.

It seemed to take forever before the *Capri*'s scanners
found the wreckage. Fragments, then ever-larger pieces,
blipped onto the screen. Slowing to avoid collision, we
circled while the ship's computer determined the exact
order and manner in which each piece was to be recov-
ered. The ship's artgrav went off, and we were weightless
again.

"It's going to take awhile to pick this up. I've never
seen a wreck so scattered," Captain Utman observed.
"Normally they implode. This looks like it was repeatedly
blasted." He kept his eyes on the screen as he spoke. I
wondered if he was fishing for information. I said nothing.

Finally metallic thumps could be heard below deck as
the ship's collector arms began retrieving pieces and putting them into the container bins in the holds.

One bin was used for organic debris. If there had been
no lights or camera in that bin, I wouldn't have guessed
that bodies were being found. As it was, after one long
look I locked off my monitor and stepped away. I really
didn't want to do this job. Having no choice, I went and
put on a pressure suit—all but the helmet.

Until the captain signaled all was ready for me, I sat
alone at the viewport and watched the many-colored
stars move as the *Capri* turned and turned again in response to the sensors' signals. No wreckage could be seen
in the blackness outside.

Please don't let me humiliate myself, was my silent,

often-repeated prayer to a god in whom I had no conscious faith. Let me do what I have to without being sick.

The SS sergeants led the way down the narrow passage over the collection bays, through the airlock and down into the bin. They carried rods to fend off floaters and guide the collection containers. After searching a body, I was to push it into its container; they would close the lid and secure the can for pickup.

My heart was beating very fast as I followed them down and tethered my safety line to a wall ring. In spite of the suit's heater, I could feel the cold of space. My old fear of pressure suits was nothing compared to being in this bin.

I'd never seen a dead person. Now they were floating all around me. Pieces of fabric, boots, and body parts drifted randomly in the cold light, bumping into walls and floating off again from their own momentum.

Most of the victims' clothing had been blown off. The bodies were mummified, freeze-dried in the vacuum of space. The brown dust settling on my visor was dried blood. Eyeballs looked like cinders in their sockets. Teeth and gums were exposed by ghastly smiles. Bones shone through parchment skin. All was so friable that it crumbled at a touch.

The data capsules were in tubes, usually in a jacket or coat pocket, although some of the women had put them in the security pouch on their belt. The belts hadn't been blown off. I checked those first, to get it over with.

A body drifted past, facedown, part of its skull missing. The camera lights glinted off something in the dusty skull cavity. Seeing Ruiz's attention diverted, I retrieved what looked like a tiny boomerang of incredibly fine fibers mounted on a hard base. Dangling from the thing were longer, heavier fibers, the thickest fine as gossamer.

Pocketing my find, I lightly tapped an elbow so that the body rolled, revealing the grotesquely distorted face of a stranger.

Then came a body still strapped to its seat, a piece of fabric draped over the head. When I took hold of the chair arm to tug it closer, the fabric drifted free. I saw then the fabric had caught on a split in the head. From that split bulged an orderly nest of optic fibers and I don't know what else. The body was an android.

I tilted the seat to see the face. It was General Burgess. The sergeants told me later that I yelled and nearly gave them all heart failure.

Then I saw Burkart lift like a balloon floating on his tether. His eyes were closed, his brown skin ashy gray with shock. Giving the general a shove that made his body ricochet off the bin wall, I caught Burkart by the arm and turned the knob on his helmet that released a spray of antitraum. Ruiz and Kim came to help, and by the time we got him up into the airlock, he was coming around.

11

WHEN I WENT BACK TO SEARCH GENERAL BUR-
gess's body, it occurred to me the android might still be
operative. For all I knew, an android's power source and
brain were in its stomach. I thought he had to have been
destroyed, but it was all I could do to make sure.

What remained of the head was so tightly packed
with ruined equipment that a cold, logical part of me
marveled at the engineering skill that had designed and
built this thing.

Was he the intended victim? And had all his copies
been "killed," too? Was this why the President sent me
on this job? Because George Burgess was *family*?

If his oldest son was an android, the President had to
be one, too. And he either assumed I knew that, or
trusted me with the knowledge. Or . . . he would have
me killed, too. And possibly the sergeants as well.

By the time Ruiz and I finished the job I'd found eight
data capsules and was shaking so much I could hardly
guide the last body into its container. I was also in danger
of being sick in my helmet, thus risking death by aspira-
tion. I'd used up all my antitraum and was very close to
panic.

The only thing that made me feel I wasn't a total weakling was that Sergeant Kim got sick when we were halfway through and had to go join Burkart. Neither had come back down.

While Ruiz and I were waiting for the airlock to open and admit us back onto the *Capri*'s deck, I saw he looked as bad as I felt.

"You used all your antitraum, too?"

He nodded. "Half an hour ago."

"Thanks for staying. I couldn't have finished without you." We were taught never to thank subordinates for doing their jobs, but I was beginning to wonder if the basis for some of the things I'd been taught was oppression, not leadership.

When I thanked him, Ruiz looked startled, then surprised me with a slow, sweet smile. "Anytime, Commander," he said. Between his smile and the airlock opening, I felt a little better.

Along with a concerned captain, Hector was waiting for me at the airlock. He took my vital signs, then gave me a shot of something calming. At my request, he gave Ruiz one, too.

"How are Kim and Burkart?" I asked the captain.

"Asleep. I gave them tranquils. It was bad down there?"

"You don't want to know, sir," Ruiz warned him.

"No," he agreed. "I don't."

Lack of time and privacy kept me from asking Hector to analyze the bristly little artifact I'd found. I was pretty sure it was an MT implant and wondered who the man was. Was his android replacement already walking somewhere? Or had it been destroyed, too?

Within an hour of signaling the President, his ships met the *Capri*. They must have been nearby, following us. If they were military craft they were unmarked: a freighter for the wreckage and the sergeants, a shuttle for Hector and me.

When I said good-bye to the sergeants, they were as subdued as they had been full of life when I first saw them, and I wondered if I would ever see them again.

Instead of a spaceport, the shuttle landed in a canyon carved by one of the ancient rivers. The place was deserted but for a waiting all-terrain vehicle, which docked itself to the shuttle hatch.

The ATV was for me only, the shuttle pilot said as he helped load Hector and my gear aboard. Since he outranked me, I assumed from his respectful manner that he knew I was on assignment for the President.

The ATV was a remote; there was no driver. Once I was aboard, it detached from the shuttle and sped away. When I looked back, the shuttle was still there, like an ornament at the end of the ATV's dust trail.

The ATV turned into a side canyon. Dark stone walls soared up on either side, narrowing the sky above to a ragged strip of stars—across which a shuttle suddenly streaked upward.

The terrain sloped. A black tunnel mouth swallowed the car, which slowed to a stop at an airlock. Dim lights came on as a hatch closed behind us. The forward hatch opened on a cavernous chamber, brightly lit.

The white floor of the cavern was parked full of ATVs, two bulldozers, and several small aircars. My car entered slowly, stopped, and announced: "Atmosphere normal. You may disembark."

I got out, wondering if I should take Hector and my gear. As I hesitated, a triangle of light appeared in the nearest wall. Out of the light walked the President, dressed as if for a formal gala. It was the first time I'd ever seen him alone. He looked smaller and—considering where I had come from—rather absurd.

"Annalyn!" He made my name sound as if I was the dearest person in the world and the one he most wanted to see. "Well done, my dear! Don't bother to kneel."

Guessing his outstretched hand wasn't a gesture of welcome, I opened my security pocket and took out the capsule tube. Before I could give it to him, he snatched it away. His hands shook as he opened it and the capsules spilled out. When I knelt to pick them up, he shoved me aside so roughly I nearly lost my balance. It was no accident, and he didn't apologize.

"Five, seven . . . eight." He counted aloud. "Yes! Correct!" And with that, he stamped the capsules to grease spots under his boot, stepped back, drew his laser pistol, and burned those greasy smears to smoke.

I was lucky to get out of the line of fire. In his shaky grip the laser beam made the stone floor bubble. He smiled the whole time. "So much for that." He reholstered his gun. "Evan was right—you were the perfect choice for this assignment. Much better than he would have been."

"Evan? You were going to send him to the *Capri*—"

"Yes, he thinks the world of you. Come along."

Evan recommended me? Because he knew I'd be safe? Or because he knew . . . I wanted to think about that but forced myself to concentrate on the President. This wasn't the time to be preoccupied about anything else.

As we walked toward that odd triangular door, I was going to tell him about George Burgess, then decided he already knew. He'd asked no questions about the people killed on the shuttle. He'd destroyed the data capsules without listening to them—meaning he knew who they came from and what they said. And he wanted no one else to know.

He'd probably ordered that shuttle destroyed. But why? And why would an android's hands shake? From emotion, or was imperfection factored in to make them seem more lifelike?

At the door he paused, half-turning to allow me to precede him, saying, "I have many enemies, you know."

I glanced up at him; he looked much more normal than he sounded.

"They're trying to get rid of me, take away my power— Get out!"

I jumped before realizing he had yelled at the Security people and aides waiting for him in the lobby we'd just entered. Grasping my arm he pulled me close, as if to protect me from them, or to use me as a shield. His grip hurt.

"Mr. President, you're needed in the control room," an aide pleaded. She was tan, intense, and wore the uniform of an SS colonel. "You must decide *now*. The city—"

"Just handle it, Colonel Haddad. Don't whine." He touched her hand, and she winced. "Remember, it's all a matter of perspective. A year from now this won't matter. In ten years most of Mars will have forgotten it. The sand buries all mistakes. And don't worry about me; I'm fine."

It seemed to me his staff wasn't worried about him but about something—at least at the moment—far more important. As I looked around at their concerned faces someone standing back by the door ducked down and slipped out. From the back he looked so much like Evan that I nearly called his name.

"But, sir," said Colonel Haddad.

"Not now!" He tugged me backward, through another door.

The door locked behind us as he hustled me along a tunnel laser-bored through the rock. The passage smelled of stone dust. Our footsteps echoed. I was so scared I nearly forgot how much my arm hurt. We stopped at a security door.

"We can speak privately in the garden," he said, opening the door to an enormous place such as I'd never seen before and never will again. How its effects were achieved I have no way of knowing, but everything in it looked, smelled, and felt *real*.

We walked beneath a rose arbor full of blooms and out onto a lawn. Wooded hills lined the horizon. Between hills and lawn flowed a river that appeared from around a rocky cliff and stretched off into the distance. Overhead was a bright blue sky where fluffy clouds floated. The lawn and flower beds sloped to the water's edge. Two odd chairs with a white table between them were placed beneath a tree.

I'd never seen a river before, only Mars's ancient, dry riverbeds. I stood staring and rubbing my bruised arm as the President walked down and settled himself in one of the chairs. After a bit he glanced back and motioned for me to join him.

"I did all the planting myself, you know," he said proudly. "What do you think of it?"

"It's wonderful," I said, and it was.

"Do you know what it is? Where it is?"

"Something copied from Earth?"

He smiled, pleased. "This is the garden behind my house back there—" He turned to point at the stone wall behind the arbor. Something about the wall disturbed him; his smile faded; his face twisted in grief. He covered his eyes with his hand and his chest heaved, as if he were trying not to cry. I looked down at the river, to spare him embarrassment. Just as abruptly, he laughed and said, "No need to be tactful. I can't cry, you know."

"I didn't know," I said when he waited for my response.

"There's no plumbing for it." He smiled again. "Too tricky even for the experts. Tear ducts aren't something you'd think you'd want. Crying would be, after all, only a gesture.''

He rested his head on the chair back, studying the horizon. ''Behind that line of trees is—was—Great Falls. On the Potomac. The river should be wider, but there wasn't enough room. Or water. This is recirculated from one of Olympia's backup reservoirs, you know. It's a small supply—it was the first one made when we learned we could melt out the permafrost.''

He turned and stared at me until I wanted to look away. ''Do you know what I am, Annalyn?''

I hesitated. ''Yes, sir. I believe you're an android with a transferred mind, sir.''

''You're sure of that?''

''Yes, sir.''

12

"*SIR?*" HE SAID SOFTLY, SADLY. "AM I A *SIR?* I remember being alive. They said I wouldn't know the difference, but I do."

He left long silences between each phrase. His expression was so strange that I wondered if they'd waited too long to transfer his original mind. He looked and sounded . . . flawed.

"Did you know when MT technology was being developed, they wanted to waste it on astronauts? So the fools could fly spaceships to nowhere and back. No point to that. You don't age at the speed of light."

For some reason that seemed to make him angry. He frowned and his mouth worked, but no words came out. When he spoke again his voice was the same, and yet it wasn't.

"I headed the Senate Appropriations Committee. Which means I controlled their research funding. So I cut them a deal: they'd get the budget they wanted and more, *if* I got what I wanted in return. And I did."

He laughed at a memory. "I made those ivory tower boys dance to my tune. After they'd done me, they said that ended our bargain; they wouldn't give Frank a transplant."

He leaned toward me, as if confiding a secret. "Frank owned Sefton-Marpack. He always made sure I never had to worry about campaign funds. I owed him big, and Wayne Hanson always pays his debts. Loyalty is what it's all about.

"They fought me on Charlie, too, so we got our ducks in a row, and with the help of the Pentagon boys, we had the whole program moved from the lab in California to the National Institute of Health, where we could keep an eye on them! I don't care how many doctorates Wu and Maddeningly had; they couldn't tell me what they would or would not do. I'd have made them do my driver if he'd been worth the bother."

He sat mumbling and chewing his lower lip while I tried to make sense of what he'd said. Hoping to jog his mind back to normal, I asked, "Where did this happen and who were you originally, sir?"

"Senator Wayne Hanson. Senior senator from Michigan. Pay attention, girl." He went on.

"By the time I—uh—*passed on*, the scientists had their act together. My new body was about thirty-five. Taller, thinner. I'd put my estate in trust for a grand-nephew—which was me, of course. That was my new identity. Nobody ever questioned it. By that time all the relatives were dead. I made sure of that. But you know, for someone as important as I'd been, my funeral was small. That was a great disappointment. People forget you."

Or maybe they remembered? I wanted to ask how

he'd "made sure" his relatives were dead, but didn't have the nerve.

"When did you come to Mars, sir?"

"On the third ship after it opened. That was Frank's idea—his company built the place. He said people died so fast up here they wouldn't be around to notice when we didn't. Here we could make 'keepers' of the people we wanted and quietly take over. He was right. Frank was a smart man."

"Are Frank and Charlie still here, sir?"

He chuckled to himself. "Frank is. Right out there." He pointed to the river. "Walked in and shorted out. He didn't like being an android. He was bored." He laughed again; I shivered. "Charlie and I cleaned up his estate and Charlie went home—he never liked Mars. We lost touch over the years . . . I can't remember what he called himself last."

"Do you look different with each new body?"

He gave me a crafty glance and hesitated before saying: "Not always. I've been Charles Reynolds a long time. This garden was on Reynolds Court. I liked the name."

"Did you give all your children MT implants?"

"Some of them."

"Gossip says all."

He didn't answer, so I asked, "If you're an android, how do you have children?"

"With great difficulty!" He laughed at his own joke. "Cryogenically frozen sperm are supposed to stay viable forever, but don't believe it. After a few—uh—unfortunate results, I used a backup system. I'm immortal, but I'm not stupid."

"So Evan and I aren't really yours?" Did Evan know this, too? Surely Janis did.

I'd gone too far. His voice dropped to a sinister whisper.

"Your genes aren't mine, but you are. I own you. I allowed you to be born. And I can make you die. Do you understand?"

"Clearly, sir. I apologize."

"Accepted."

His voice became suddenly, eerily normal again, as if fading reception had been restored. "I can understand your curiosity. In your place I'd ask the same questions."

He sat up, hyper-alert. "Do you know what's missing? Birds! Bluejays. Mockingbirds. Those little black-capped . . . chickadees. And squirrels . . ." His glance fell on me, and he frowned, as if he didn't know how I'd gotten there. "They all belong here, you know."

"If you say so, sir."

"Don't humor me," he warned, then added in a clinical tone, "I just had the urge to kill you . . . whoever you are. I must take care of that."

He sat up straighter and twisted in his chair. I froze, thinking he was going to draw his gun and shoot me. Why had I left Hector in the car!

Then, to my immense relief, he sighed and settled back. "I have to remember . . . you're young. You never lived off-Mars. Certainly never here in Virginia."

"No, sir."

"No . . . The bad part of being MT'd is after a while there's no one left who shares your memories. You're all alone inside your mind." He looked over at me. "Are you afraid, Annalyn?"

"Yes, sir." He knew me again!

"Me, too." He nodded agreement. "What are you afraid of?"

"You. That you're going to kill me."

"Really?" His surprise seemed real. "Why would I do that? You're the only one of my children who's never asked for a favor. I'm going to keep you safe here with me."

"Thank you." He'd apparently forgotten wanting to kill me a few seconds before. "What are we keeping safe from, sir?"

"The past." He leaned across the table to confide. "Do you know what's even worse than being alone? Dreams. I used to have such nice dreams. Now they're all bad. Sometimes I'm running—"

His speech garbled. His hands began to shake so much his fingernails clicked on the metal chair arms. Looking at those hands as if they belonged to someone else, he tried to regain control by clasping them tightly together and trapping them between his knees.

"This unit . . . tampered with. Enemies!" he said, ". . . must . . . Tampered with."

With a spastic upward motion he managed to yank open his tunic collar. That accomplished, his arms dropped as if they were dead weights hanging from his shoulders.

Taking a deep breath, he stiffened. Suddenly the right hand flew up and karate-chopped the head so hard I cried out at the sound. His head snapped back and hung at an impossible angle; he went limp and started to slide out of the chair. His eyes rolled back until only the whites showed. His mouth fell open, and from him came a sound like air hissing from a balloon.

"Mr. President!"

At that moment the ground shook violently. As if in slow motion his chair tipped sideways, his weight shifted, and he tumbled out onto the grass. The impact forced another *chuff* of air from him. Water slopped and swirled around my legs as I knelt beside him.

The ground shook again. Part of the lawn dropped and tore open in a ragged gash, revealing soil and pipes. Water rushed into the gash, bringing the smell of fresh mud and bruised grass.

"Leave it! We've got to get out of here."

I jumped to my feet. There beneath the arbor stood the President, or an exact copy, complete to the same dress uniform. I looked down at the body and felt myself sway.

"Get up here!" He came running down the lawn and I thought he was coming for me, but he wasn't. He wanted the pistol and belt from his *old* body. Yanking it free, he set the gun on high and blasted the old android into ash and twisted metal. Whatever was in the thing stank as it burned.

I struggled up the slope. At a particularly bad jolt I looked back to see the river sloshing from side to side like water about to spill from a bowl. Trees were swaying; some had fallen. Thick, black strings of carbon floated in the now-hazy sunlight. The ground quaked so hard I fell into the rose arbor, and thorns scratched me when I freed myself.

"Keep going," the President called, putting on the pistol belt as he caught up with me. When he opened the door to the tunnel, so much dust and wind swirled in that he had to close it again and blink his eyes.

"What's happening?" I wiped grit from my face and hair.

"I think we're being bombed," he said calmly. "They're trying to scare me into stepping aside, letting them run things. But Mars is my business. I own the most shares; I make the decisions. And I must have the power to enforce them. The master computer takes care of the rest. Nobody's hungry—"

"Who are *they?*"

"Traitors. Commoners who claim they want a democracy; elites who want a bigger profit share. But the attack here is George's doing. He's the only one who could have told them where to find me. Told the ships the codes to get past our defense system. This is personal. Payback."

"For blowing up the ship from Phobos?"

"Yes . . ."

"But General Burgess is—a copy?"

"No." The President smiled with satisfaction. "*You*

saw the last of George. He never had any sense of loyalty. George and his brother always took everything I gave them for granted. So I took it all back."

"Weren't he and the others on that ship from Phobos just coming here to talk?"

"They were coming to make demands. No one makes demands to me."

"But if they're dead— Who's attacking?"

"If I knew their names, they'd be dead, too! Come on!"

He pushed me out into the tunnel, let the door close behind him, and touched the ID lock. "You'll forget this place. What happened. Everything I might have said. Do you understand?"

Before I could answer, frantic aides, some in surface suits and all of them in helmets, came running down the tunnel in full cry.

They put helmets on us and hurried us out to the cavern where the ATVs waited. The cold and dust in that big chamber were a shock. Through the window in the airlock I could see the outer hatch wedged half open and rocks from the canyon spilling inside. The ground kept trembling, and the equipment parked on the floor rattled and swayed on its suspensions.

An alarm rang as a second triangular hatch in the left wall of the cavern opened, revealing a strange tubular vehicle.

"Shall we go?" The President offered me his arm, as if he were going to escort me to dinner.

"I need my things from the car." As I ran toward the

ATV, Hector opened the car door and hopped to the floor. He was carrying my rollbag.

"Forget the robot! We don't have time," called the President.

I ignored him. There was no way I was going to leave Hector to be buried there. Hector was more human than most people. Certainly more human than the President.

13

THE CAR SHOT ALONG THE TUNNEL LIKE A BULLET
through a gun barrel. There were no windows; we might
have been in space but for the sense of speed. The President sat alone on the front seat. The rest of us were
crammed into rows behind him. Hector was on my lap.
Our helmets made us look like bubbleheads.

Numbed by fear and lack of sleep, I didn't know
where we were going, or where we'd been, and didn't
much care.

I was wakened by a whooshing noise and a computer
saying, "Eagle's Nest. Atmosphere, normal. Security,
normal."

I was alone in the car with Hector. The hatch was
open on a green-carpeted platform. I couldn't hear a
sound even after taking my helmet off. The air felt cold.

The station platform became a tunnel curving back to
end in a dim, low-ceilinged space. One wall was full of
electronic equipment. On the other was a window deeply
recessed into the stone and so dark it may have been a
periscope.

Everyone was crowded around the window, watching what appeared to be colored lights flashing outside.
Officers urgently whispered to their computers.

By standing on tiptoe and peering around heads, I could see out. We were somewhere high up in the crater rim, looking down on Olympia. Then with a rush of horror I realized all the pretty lights were laser fire. Olympia was under aerial attack!

I remembered Colonel Haddad asking him to make a decision about the city when he and I walked in from that cavern. And he'd told her to "handle it." Then he'd spent all that time talking to me while *this* was going on? Why? Was his android defective—or was he plain crazy? Didn't he care about living people? Thousands were down there. Shala was down there!

From emplacements hidden in the crater rim and floor, laser cannon fired solid-looking beams of red and yellow. From the darkness overhead, the attackers shot back blue and green. If a beam hit a crystal shield just right, jewel-like sparkles went dancing across the city and up the crater walls.

"Sonar cannon!" a voice cried. "Coming in on landers!"

"They're targeting everything but Midtown, Mr. President."

"Try to blast the cannon before they land," he ordered.

Then I understood: this was a command post. His urgently whispering officers were directing the defense of the city. Had our automated system been sabotaged by George Burgess or the people Shala was worried about?

In the dark the sonar cannon weren't visible until they landed and went rolling up to their targets. We had studied these weapons in class, but I truly didn't know what those ominous vehicles could do until they all pulsed in unison.

Within seconds sound waves too low for human hearing surged through the stone. Sound entered my feet, pushed up my legs, and socked me in the stomach. As if I were being squeezed to death, I couldn't breathe; my heart faltered painfully before thumping into beat again. Sharp pain shot from my ears to my throat, and I groaned and staggered, nearly falling with vertigo.

My vision blurred. When I could partially see again, the first thing I noticed was everyone looked as scared as I was. Some were stumbling around, disoriented. Others knelt by the fallen. I helped several to their feet. Their mouths moved, but I could hear only the painfully loud ringing in my ears.

The President had ripped open his tunic and was frantically adjusting something where his heart should have been. Thin red liquid, like transmission fluid, ran from his ears and nose. He mopped it away with his sleeves.

"You are in great danger." Hector's voice seemed to come from far away. "You should not be here. Repeat, you are in great danger. I cannot protect you from sound."

He was right, but I didn't know where else to go. Luckily the window had held. When my vision cleared, I saw many of the city's smaller shields were shattering.

The pink dome over the Imaji Hotel was the first to go, crazing to opacity before collapsing into a ringdune of sand. The hotel stood naked in the ruin. The spaceport terminal fell next, and suddenly we were looking down on exposed waiting areas, with nothing between the tiny rows of chairs and the sandy crater floor outside. Then the most beautiful shield of all—The Fountains—turned to yellow-gold amber and slowly crumbled inward, from the top down.

Exposed to the gray Martian sky, everything that lived beneath those shields gasped for life like goldfish thrown from the bowl. Bodies lay everywhere, scattered like bright bits of confetti.

Mist clouds formed above the pools and fountains, quickly froze, and fell as snow. Here and there aircars took off. Some escaped; others were hit by laser fire and crashed.

A blue beam hit the Sanctuary. Fire flashed on the roof and immediately died for lack of oxygen. Tiny figures came running out and fell in the courtyards.

When a beam struck Fountain House, the president groaned softly. I glanced up at him. He was expressionless; only his eyes moved, like a camera recording the scene. He's a machine, I reminded myself; what else can you expect of him—it.

But to be honest, at the time I remember feeling almost nothing. That my secure world and everyone in it could be destroyed so quickly was beyond comprehension. I was seeing it happen, but it didn't seem real. Perhaps the same was true for him.

"Did they have any warning, sir?" I had to repeat the question twice before he heard me.

"Some," he said vaguely. "They were told to go down into the transport tunnels." He looked at me, as if wondering how I got there. "Your robot's right. I'll speak with Colonel Haddad about getting you out of here."

"Sir, with your permission, I should report to the emergency center in Midtown, if that's possible. If that shield holds, they'll need all the trained emergency people—"

"Midtown can take care of itself. The traitors—"

"Shala's down there! She's—"

"Colonel?" He whispered something to her; she nodded and spoke to her pocket computer. "This way, Annalyn." He led me out into the hallway. Hector followed.

"I really want to go to Midtown, sir. Shala was my companion and she's—"

"If she's not safe, it's too late now. Listen closely. There's not much time." His voice dropped to a conspiratorial whisper. "You're the only one of my children I trust. More importantly, the only one I respect. Someday you'll take my place. You'll be my heir—you need great wealth in this position, for security if nothing else—"

"Thank you, sir. I'm honored but—"

"Just listen! Regardless of what you think you know, I don't want to rule forever. But, until I formally retire, this is our secret. If you repeat to anyone what I just said, I'll have you killed and your copy deleted."

He paused, perhaps to let the threat sink in, but only one thing had made an impression on me.

"You're saying I do have an MT implant?"

"Yes."

"Does Evan?"

"Yes."

"Are there androids of us?"

"No. You're too young. Besides, the bodies are standard. Only head and hands are customized on most models. For now you are only mind copies, growing like lovely crystals in the darkness." Seeing me shudder, he frowned. "Doesn't that please you? I've made you immortal."

"Look how happy it's made you."

For a moment he looked angry but then gave me a wry smile. "You say that because you're young. Death has no reality for you yet. But believe me, hundreds of people down there in the city would have given anything for the gift I gave you. Someday you'll be grateful, too."

He turned to leave, then paused to pat me on the shoulder and said, "Make me proud—"

"Mr. President? Father?"

At the sound of Evan's voice we both spun around. There he stood behind us, somehow managing to look jaunty even in a pressure suit, his left arm crooked over his bubble helmet.

I was so glad to see him in the midst of all this that I hugged him before remembering. "That *was* you back there. Why did you recommend me for . . . space duty, and why are you here, with the President? You said . . ."

At his disapproving frown I fell silent, wondering what bounds I'd overstepped, or what security I'd breached.

"Hello, Annie." Ignoring my questions, he freed himself with a quick smile and turned to the President. "I'm sorry, sir, but you're needed in the Command Center."

"Why didn't you page me? How long were you eavesdropping?"

Evan didn't seem bothered by the President's obvious anger. "I was told to come get you, sir. I was following orders."

"How much did you overhear?"

"Your final phrase, sir. I believe you wanted Annie to make you proud?"

The President's eyes never left Evan's face as he said, "Annalyn, go see if Haddad has your new orders ready."

"Yes, sir." As I walked away, I heard him tell Evan: "You're here because Janis . . ." He lowered his voice then, but I'd heard enough to guess the rest.

Colonel Haddad met me with, "You look exhausted, Commander." Before I could dodge away, she grasped my chin and broke an antitraum capsule in my face. As the minty scent wafted up my nose she leaned close to whisper, "Take this with you, just in case." She gave me a drug packet along with a disposable recorder containing my orders. "I must walk you to the car."

"To make sure I go?"

She didn't smile. "To program your destination."

We passed Evan and the President on the way. Totally absorbed in listening to the President, Evan didn't so much as glance my way.

Haddad typed codes into the bullet car's controls.

"This will deliver you to a subway station annex some distance from the city. Your orders will tell you where you go from there."

"Are the trains still running?"

She permitted herself a slight smile at that. "The master computer reports no problems with trains at that station."

14

As the capsule car sped downhill, I sat in the President's seat, listening to my orders—which made no sense at all. I was to go to Itek—where Evan had said he was going.

"For the duration of the emergency, you will serve as the North District's military governor," the orders said. "You also will assume responsibility for the safety and comfort of the First Lady and other elite refugees from Olympia temporarily housed there."

"I've never been an administrator," I said aloud to Hector. "Why did he give me this job?"

"I cannot answer your question," said Hector.

"I don't expect you to," I said irritably. "I'm just thinking out loud. And why is Evan with him? Why not send him to Itek with his mother?" The idea of having to deal with Janis was depressing. If she was at Itek, she'd never accept my authority.

I rested my head against the cushion. My arms and legs felt like lead. I needed sleep and food and something to drink. My eyes burned, but just as I closed them, the car's computer announced: "Approaching station twenty-one. Station twenty-one. Prepare to disembark."

As soon as the car stopped, the door hissed open onto

a narrow, brightly lit platform leading to a security door. The cold air smelled of stone. The floor was thick with dust.

"We're here," I told Hector, wondering where "here" was. Leaning over to pick up my rollbag, a wave of dizziness warned me I better eat soon.

As soon as Hector hopped out onto the platform behind me, the car closed its door and eased back into the dark tunnel, going back the way it came. Somewhere an airlock sealed; a muffled *whoosh* shook the platform, and then there was total silence.

At our approach the platform door opened reluctantly, as if there was grit in the runners. The light beyond was dim. Bits of rubble tumbled through the opening; there was more debris on the floor outside.

I had expected to enter a normal station of the Inner City subway line. Instead the place looked as if it had been bombed. There was a chemical smell in the air.

One good look and the adrenaline of fear removed all trace of sleepiness. Fumbling for my pocket communicator, I tried to call Colonel Haddad. The only sound from my communicator was white noise. I pressed EMER-GENCY. White noise. Nothing responded.

Any hope of escape had just departed at high speed. I was alone with a robot in a bombed-out subway station somewhere deep under the Martian surface, hungry, and in sudden need of a sanit.

My mind was racing: was this a mistake or deliberate? Did the President know about this? Did Colonel Haddad —I opened my rollbag and looked in the drug packet.

She'd given me enough antitraum to calm Midtown. Or to kill myself, if I used enough of it at once. A humanitarian gesture?

Looking around at the wreckage I remembered asking her if the trains were running. She hadn't said yes. And she had smiled.

The more I thought about it, the more I went from being scared to being really angry. After successfully completing a terrible assignment for the President, *this* was my reward? I grabbed the nearest piece of rock and threw it. The effort of throwing made me dizzy, and the rock landed with a feeble crash somewhere in the dark. There wasn't even an echo.

Something about that feeble noise made me understand: how or why I got here didn't matter at the moment. What mattered was getting out of here—survival —and getting mad or feeling sorry for myself wasn't going to help.

I looked around, took a deep, slow breath, and exhaled. Deep breathing wasn't as good as antitraum, but it helped. There was adequate atmosphere. Which meant the damage didn't go all the way to the surface. I tried my communicator again, then carefully put it into the rollbag with the drug packet.

Beside me Hector turned slowly, beeping to himself, and then announced, "The area is stable. Exercising due caution, we may proceed."

"Good. Let's see what we can find."

After checking to make sure nothing would fall on us from overhead, we stepped out into what was left of the station. The door tried to close behind us but jammed halfway.

The track wells were full of debris, the biggest pieces from a partially collapsed ramp to an upper level. A walkway ended in midair; the ceiling behind it had fallen. Somewhere in the stillness water was slowly dripping.

The dust had settled, which meant the damage had happened hours before—or the vent fans had gone on working. And I couldn't see any bodies. Did it happen late at night, or was this station closed before the explosion?

There was light in a side hallway from four built-in food dispensers that looked almost undamaged. The hallway led to the public sanits. Across from the food dispensors was a row of phone booths!

None of the phones worked—which I should have guessed by seeing their broken vu-screens. A large hope died.

I sent Hector in to check the sanit. He reported it safe. Only the cold water worked. Washing my hands and face seemed to be the first reality I'd experienced in days. I washed my hands twice just to smell the soap. The hot air drying jets didn't work.

Hector was waiting for me when I came out. "The destruction was caused by explosives placed in nine separate locations," he announced.

"How do you know?"

"Chemical traces of explosives linger in nine locations."

"Is anyone else alive down here?"

"My sensors detect no human sound or movement. There is organic decomposition. Do you wish to know the sources?"

"Spoiled food?"

"No. Human."

"I don't want to see."

Two of the food dispensers still worked. I ate a hot sandwich so fast I burned my mouth and didn't care. Still hungry, I used my credit ID again for more sandwiches and orange juice, and sat down on a fallen rock slab to eat. Unwrapping my third sandwich, it occurred to me that this was the first meal I'd enjoyed all week. Which made me laugh, and then the tears came.

Once I started crying I couldn't stop. Somehow crying allowed me to accept the truth: I'd been sent here to die. I'd seen and heard too much. My orders made no sense because I was never supposed to reach Itek.

While seeming so concerned, my father—who wasn't my father—had lied about wanting to keep me safe. Olympia was being attacked *now*, but the bombs in this station had been detonated hours before. And unless the master computer was malfunctioning, he and his colonel knew that.

Did Evan know? He knew about the *Capri*. That thought gave me a cold stab in my stomach, and almost instantly I dismissed it as impossible. I was being paranoid.

"You are crying," said Hector. "Are you in pain?"

"Not physically."

"Why are you crying?"

"Because I just figured out that we were sent here to die."

Hector didn't answer with his usual speed. "By *to die*, do you mean a total shutdown of all functions?"

"Correct."

"How would that happen?"

"I'll freeze to death. Or starve."

"You initially said *we*. Why will I cease functioning?"

"You won't," I admitted, "but you'll be trapped here until a repair crew arrives. That could take weeks."

"How would a repair crew arrive?" asked Hector.

"Through the tunnels, once they're reopened."

"Are the tunnels completely closed?" asked Hector. "We have not checked."

"Yes, but I . . . You're right!" Hope began to return. I grinned at Hector, then hiccupped from crying and eating too fast. "It's good to have you to remind me of things I should have thought of myself. Thank you."

"You are welcome."

Wiping my face with the napkins from the sandwich packet, I left the sandwich with my rollbag and set off to explore.

There was no way I could get to the upper level without a rope and grappling hook. From atop a broken beam near the ramp I peered down into the rail wells. Two bodies were almost hidden down there. One still wore part of a uniform; a shiny white arm badge reflected light. Their boots were gone, and their feet looked charred.

The academy had taught us the theories of war but nothing of how people died. The only thing that saved me from losing my lunch was Hector saying, "There is a map on the board leaning against that I beam, approximately ten feet seven inches to your left."

Swallowing the sourness, I crawled over and tugged a subway wall map back into the light by the food dispensers.

The capsule car had called this "station twenty-one," which meant nothing to me, but when I saw the name WIND CANYON on the map, I knew when we were.

With an x'd YOU ARE HERE, the color-coded map showed Wind Canyon was the first stop outside of Olympia, some thirty miles east of Midtown. On the lower level, where I was, the trains went on to Regis, a hundred miles to the east. By going up the ramp, one could transfer to the trains that went north to Zion or south to Redwall.

Looking at the map, it seemed logical that this station had been destroyed to seal off Olympia. But who had done it, and why? The rebels, to keep the President from escaping? Or the President, to contain the rebels and keep others from joining them? Not that it mattered at the moment.

"OK," I told Hector, "if we can get into one of the westbound tunnels—and walk thirty miles—I know the way home."

15

CLIMBING HALFWAY UP THE RUBBLE, I COULD SEE the eastbound tunnel was thoroughly sealed shut, but the westbound entrance had possibilities. I climbed toward the west.

Using a broken steel rod as a pry bar, I carefully rolled away pieces of stone and concrete until there was a hole big enough to see through.

A few dim platform lights showed rubble spilled out into the tunnel in a long slope. The light ended with the platform. If I could get Hector down there and past the debris, we'd still have to walk thirty miles in the dark.

So that I could get Hector through, I made the hole twice as big as I needed, then carefully crawled back to where he waited. Cold as it was in there, I was sweating.

"I'm going to go wash," I told him. My uniform was ruined, but I saw no point in changing. "When I get back, I'll put some sandwiches and drinks into my pack and we can go."

"When will you sleep?" he asked. "According to my timer, we are well into your normal sleep period."

Surprised, I checked my watch. It was one in the morning. "It's too cold to sleep here. I'd freeze to death.

Besides, I'm afraid to stay here any longer than we have to."

Over his protests I stuffed Hector into my rollbag and adjusted the straps to wear it as a backpack, leaving his "head" peering over my shoulder.

Ripping out a piece of jacket lining, I soaked the fabric in the water dripping from a drink dispenser and tied it over my face to keep out some of the stone dust. The wet rag in the cold of the station made me shiver.

After a certain point on the rubble mound it was hard to climb without scraping Hector off. Getting through the hole was worse. I finally managed to twist around and go through sideways. By the time we reached the tunnel floor I was sweating again, my hands and knees all scraped and bleeding. It didn't matter. We were out of the station!

"Illumination is inadequate," said Hector. Without warning a small cone of bright light shot over my shoulder and swept a circle across the red rock tunnel walls. "Hector Protectors are equipped to serve in all situations."

"How long will your light last?"

"My power cell is designed for twenty years of normal use. As I have been underutilized in your service, I anticipate no power shortage. Unless you walk very slowly."

"I thought robots had no sense of humor."

"I was stating fact, not attempting to amuse."

The tunnel was kidney-shaped with a rounded roof, the floor two half-curves with the float rail down the center. Laser-cut, the glazed rock was slippery. Hector's weight threw me off balance so that my feet tended to slide. Fear of falling and hurting myself or damaging Hector forced me to walk a slow, straight line.

I don't know what I would have done without his light. I couldn't have walked even a mile in the pitch black without panicking because the wall was too far away to touch and the float rail too low. The only sounds down there were my footsteps and my blood pulsing in my ears.

I lost all sense of time. Exhaustion made me spacey. When I sat down to rest and eat, my legs shook from tension. Rest stops became more frequent, but I couldn't sit long for fear of falling asleep and freezing. To keep awake I worried about what I might find when we reached the city.

What if the Central Station had been bombed and we were trapped down here? What if we got to Midtown safely and I was shot by guards watching to see if I showed up? When fear no longer kept me awake, Hector did—with everything from noise to small electrical shocks.

After fifteen hours, Hector's light began to pick up more dust. The air seemed warmer and something smelled bad.

"What stinks?"

"Decomposing organic waste," said Hector.

"What exactly does that mean?"

"Humans."

"Where?"

"Near."

"Dead?"

"No."

It was hard to know whether to be glad or scared but I was so tired I didn't much care. Hector's light swept the tunnel. It revealed no people or waste but showed the tunnel widened to accommodate a railed catwalk on the right-hand side.

At the first rail post I lifted Hector up onto the catwalk and with great effort pulled myself up after him. Being on a level, nonslippery surface seemed a great luxury. I lay on that cold floor for minutes, my legs trembling, too exhausted to stand.

Once I caught my breath and could move again, I saw a metal sign on the wall at the end of the catwalk. NO PERSONNEL ALLOWED BEYOND THIS POINT it said.

We went on, Hector leading the way now, lighting up the floor and right wall. The stench grew more disgusting.

At the end of a long, slow curve we came upon a train sitting in the tunnel like a huge metal worm dead in its burrow. The odd thing was, the train seemed endless; car after car had been sealed together. The walkway was now a narrow hall, with one wall made of curving metal plates with accordion joints.

"Hector, stop."

There was a sound other than the squeak of his feet in the dust. For a long moment there was silence and then I heard muffled voices from the train. There were people inside!

I wanted to hammer on the car and shout, Hey, we made it! But I didn't. If people were living in the trains, conditions in what was left of the city were pretty bad, possibly lawless. There was no point in letting anyone know I was out here.

"Danger!"

Hector shut off his light and stopped so quickly I nearly fell over him. Only a wild grab and luck saved me from kicking him into the train. For a moment all was darkness and panic. Then, while setting him upright again, I saw what had made him stop. There was light ahead. We'd reached the station.

There were people on the catwalk up ahead, black profiles against the distant light. Some sat hunched against the wall; others lay on the cement.

A man got to his feet, stepped over a sleeper, and peed against the nearest train car. In the backlight a faint white mist of steam rose from the warm liquid. The man turned and sat down again.

This bold act of civil disobedience shocked me. That anyone would dare to disobey sanitation codes, to say nothing about the laws against wasting recyclable liquids, must mean that what was left of the city was in chaos.

Never mind that I had twice committed the same crime in the tunnel. I'd had no choice. This man was close to the station's sanits.

When Hector and I walked out of the darkness no one seemed surprised, even a little. They showed no curiosity. No one spoke. Few even looked at us. As if numb beyond all caring, they simply moved aside to let us pass.

"Is the attack over?" I waited until I was on the station platform to ask. I had to ask four people before a woman roused herself enough to say, "I guess so."

"Is Midtown still secure?"

"I guess so." She sniffed and gave a shrug. "If you call this secure." The sweep of her arm took in the scene.

The doors were open on the trains inside the station. All the seats were full; people sat in the aisles. They looked apathetic, as if overdosed with antitraum. A few glanced my way, but none made eye contact.

The architectural beauty of Olympia's Midtown Central Station was a cruel contrast to the crowds of refugees it housed. Shaped like a cross, the building was bright with cream and yellow glo-paint. Boxed trees grew ceiling high. Red flowers tumbled from planters. Tiny lights glittering in the high ceiling suggested friendly stars.

In the wide halls that formed the arms of the cross and led to the train platforms, rows of tube-frame bunk beds, four tiers high, had been set up. Most were occupied, although it was only late afternoon.

In the Grand Hall crowds of people stood about or sat in ragged islands. Toddlers wandered unsupervised, some crying fretfully, all of them dirty. On one side of the room children played a joyless game of catch with a wad of paper.

The odor I'd noticed in the tunnel was much worse up here, a stink of unwashed bodies and human waste. Clearly there was a water shortage. Long lines waited to use the sanits.

Security officers patroled the lines, keeping order,

giving preference to children. Each time an officer escorted a child to the front of the line, waiting adults yelled abuse, made threatening remarks, or just grumbled.

Instead of train schedules, the ARRIVAL and DEPARTURE screens ran endless lists of names in alphabetical order. Each name was followed by a location: *John Smith, MedCen & Avenue A & 4th St.*

"If you haven't registered at the census desk, please do so now," a loudspeaker blared. "The desk is located under the blinking yellow light in the Grand Hall. If you're searching for a loved one, please see the information screens. Shelter lists are updated at ten-minute intervals. Thank you."

"That means you." I whirled around as a station security guard tapped me on the shoulder. "It's OK," he said. "Don't be scared. I saw you and the robot come in. I'd bet you're not on the survivors' list yet, are you?" He gave me what was meant to be a reassuring smile.

I shook my head, trying to think. If I registered, the President would know where I was. But if I tried to escape, I'd just attract attention and the guard would catch me anyhow because I was too tired to run.

The guard took hold of my elbow. "It's OK." His calming voice suggested he thought my hesitation meant I was in shock—maybe I was. "I'll walk you and your robot to the desk. They'll take care of you."

16

AT THE CENSUS DESK, THE OFFICERS ON DUTY looked surprised and none too happy to see me. Their faces were dirty, their eyes red with fatigue. The man said, "Is that an honor guard uniform?"

I glanced down at myself. "What's left of it."

"It's yours?" asked the woman.

"Yes." What an odd question.

"So where's the President?" he asked.

"I don't know." Which was true.

"But if you're a commander in his honor guard—"

"I don't know."

He gave me a long, skeptical look, then grudgingly said, "Right hand on the ID plate."

They exchanged glances when my face and ID came on-screen. "She's one of his kids." The woman pressed a button. "We'll keep her off the survivors' list."

My stomach knotted tighter. Was there an order out for my arrest? "Why are you doing that, Corporal?" I tried not to let my voice shake.

"For your protection." Sounding apologetic, she explained, "The President isn't popular right now. People know he left town before the emergency. Along with the Council and most of the elites. People think the rich all knew what was coming and left us here to die. We had no warning—"

"What are you doing here, Commander?" the man interrupted her. "The screen says you're on off-Mars assignment."

"I came back in time to get trapped in a transport tunnel," I said, relieved that they didn't seem to have a warrant for me. "Not to change the subject, but is there a quick way to find out where someone is?"

"My guess is anyone left in your area's dead," he said with unnecessary bluntness. "You may not know it, but The Fountains took a lot of hits. The whole shield's *gone*."

"I know," I said, ignoring his attempt to shock me, "but I'd appreciate your checking to see if Shala Parvez and Kati—Katya—Assam are among the survivors."

"Watch the screens, like everybody else."

"We can do it for her." The woman gave her partner a warning look, a reminder that even now he had to be careful not to insult an elite. Turning to me with an apologetic smile she asked, "What were those names?"

I knew by her expression what was coming when she said, "They're not on the survivors' list. I'll check casualties." Endless seconds passed. She looked up again. "I'm sorry. Sergeant Katya Assam's body was found outside the academy."

I expected it, and yet I didn't. "And Shala?"

"Shala Parvez is listed as a Midtown resident but her body was found at the Sanctuary."

"That can't be right! The computer's wrong!"

"The ID was clear. Maybe she was visiting a friend?"

I didn't answer. All I could think was: she can't be dead. How could that be? Shala? Why would she be out there? All her friends lived in Midtown now. Unless someone invited her there . . . told her I was there . . . Could that have happened? Because she was my friend and I might have told her about being sent to the *Capri?*

"I'm sorry, Commander. Is there someone else we can contact? Perhaps a family member?" Her voice was gentle now.

I remember staring at her right shoulder.

"Commander? Are you all right?"

When I still didn't respond, she got up, took my hand, led me to the VIP lounge, told me to rest awhile, and left. They had other people waiting and I was blocking the desk. My tragedy was their commonplace.

In spite of the crowd outside, the VIP lounge was empty, the thick carpets, soft chairs, and sofas unused, the sanit mine alone. As if there was no emergency great enough to allow commoners into an elite facility.

I sat on the edge of a sofa and wondered why I wasn't crying. Shala was dead, and all I felt was empty, numb. And guilt that it was probably because of me that she had died.

Hector stood beside me, silent. I stared down at him and slowly understood why all those people outside looked and acted so numb, too.

With no warning, what seemed like a bolt of lightning flashed inside my head. I "saw" the lightning, although that's impossible. What wasn't quite pain spidered back and forth over my skull. I reached up to clasp my head and felt myself falling. Hector said, "Annalyn?" The room went black.

Voices woke me. I opened my eyes and closed them against painfully bright light. A stranger's voice said, "Wake up, Annalyn. You've slept too long. You need solid food and some exercise." A firm hand patted my cheek until I opened one eye just enough to see out. This was someplace new.

"I'm awake," I muttered, brushing the hand away.

"Good. The guards couldn't wake you yesterday," the voice explained. "They brought you here to the MedCen. We couldn't find anything wrong that rest couldn't help, so we put in an IV to feed you and let you sleep. How do you feel?"

Then I remembered . . . Shala was dead! And this man had never heard of her and wouldn't care.

"OK. Fine." I moved my arm and tape tugged at my skin.

"Hold still." He deftly, painlessly pulled a needle out of my left arm. "You were pretty dehydrated." With a tug of tape, cold air flooded the patch of skin that had been covered. "Sit up. Slowly. Good."

Squinting against the light I saw a small brown man with wiry salt-and-pepper hair and a pleasant face. A badge on his uniform ID'd him as JAMES STEVENS, MEDTEC.

"It's none of my business," he said, "but I've got to ask—and you don't have to answer—since you're the President's daughter, how did you end up in danger? I mean, anybody who was *anybody* got out of town long before things got blasted. Just us poor dumb commoners were caught here."

"Is that true?"

He grinned, as if delighted by my innocence. "From what I hear, the President even had the factories sealed up safe and sound beforehand. Protected the moneymakers. Now for the commoners' benefit, they did call a medical emergency drill. Got us all in here. None of us knew what kind of emergency we were supposed to be practicing. But your kind of people were long gone by the time the news said there was *some* danger of the city being attacked and people should go down into the tunnels, *just in case.*" He laughed at those words.

"Are you sure? That's how it happened?"

"Of course I'm sure, girl." The question irked him. "If you're here, why don't you know that?"

"It's a long story, Mr. Stevens. Where's Hector? My robot? He was with me. He—"

"He's under your bed." The medtec shook his head. "Pushy little thing. I never had a robot plug into *my* systems to approve the treatment *my* patient was going to get. I was afraid he'd blow my head off."

"Hector wouldn't do that."

"He threatened—he warned me. Kept saying he was your protector. Monitoring your safety." Stephens grinned. "He's a pretty good medtech. I could use him here."

"He's a Protector robot. My mother gave him to me."

"Did she now?" Stevens looked from me to Hector.

"Well, I guess she knew you might need him," he said thoughtfully. "If you got left behind here . . . Life is probably a little risky in the rarefied air you elite folks breathe."

"What does that mean?"

"Well . . . the rumor is, the President had the subways shut down to keep us Midtown riffraff from leaving. Like we were all rebels and had to be contained. So how and why did you get left behind with us?"

When I didn't answer he gave a cynical chuckle. "Whatever you are, Annalyn Court, if the President wants to get rid of you, you can't be all bad."

He picked up a pocket flash lying on the bed and put it into his breast pocket. "Got to go. Lots more patients to see. You wait for your breakfast and you eat it all. No wasting. Food's in short supply."

When he opened the door I realized for the first time I was given special treatment by having a private room. Rows of beds, end-to-end, lined both sides of the hallway outside. All were occupied.

"What's wrong with them?" I asked, shocked by the sight.

"Heart. Lungs. Ears—lots of that. Laser burns. Glass cuts. Abrasions. Trauma." A thought distracted him. "Oh, I almost forgot, a General Offrey called. He said he'd come get you. You want me to let him know you can leave?"

"Please. He's the commandant of the academy. How did he . . . ?"

"Live through it? Who knows?" He shrugged and raised his hand in a mock salute. "You be careful out there, Annalyn Court. Some people might want to make you answer for your father's actions. Don't count too much on that robot."

17

GENERAL OFFREY ARRIVED IN CIVILIAN CLOTHES.
"We'll talk in the car," he said. Hector and I followed him in silence through the crowded halls and out.

The MedCen is next to a park. To smell trees and grass again was wonderful. For the first time in days I could see outside through the shield. Above the crater rim, far off to the north, the wind whipped dust plumes miles into the gray-pink sky. I took a deep breath, grateful to be alive.

No shops were open, but people were standing around, as if waiting for something to happen. Some were looking at us and the car, and they didn't look too friendly.

"Are they waiting for news about patients in the MedCen?" I asked, but all the general said was, "Get in!"

Both he and his car were so spotlessly clean that I tried to dust off Hector and my rollbag before stowing them behind the seat.

"Not *now*." The general impatiently tossed in my bag and set Hector on top of it. "Get in before your uniform provokes an incident." He slammed the door behind me.

After telling the car's computer our destination—the

Midtown Federal Building—he put his pistol on the seat between us.

"Is it that dangerous?" I asked.

"Possibly." The car began to move. "People are angry. Understandably so. Their government allowed this to happen and then deserted them."

"But what exactly happened?"

"I don't know *exactly*," he said. "Obviously the object of the attack was the President—to end his dictatorship. Obviously a large group of the elite knew what was coming and fled. Various factions have been trying to institute a democracy for years. The President's response has always been to kill the opposition. This time he failed."

"But how would our own people get armed spaceships? And sonar cannon?"

He gave me a surprised glance. "How do you know about those?" When I didn't answer, he said, "Exactly. I believe rebels supplied the necessary data—some are elites whom he's exiled over the years—but Mars was attacked by mercenaries."

"Mercenaries?"

"Hired professionals. But to hire such a force costs far more than any group of rebel commoners could afford. Thus I suspect some of Mars's customers are involved, that they provided the financial backing. And that they were convinced to do so by specific members of the elite class."

"General Burgess?"

"He could be among them. Certainly he would be

pleased to take his father's place. And the financial back-
ers would have been able to negotiate better, more profitable terms on Mars's exports with him as President.''

I thought that over and decided it made sense. Did
Janis know about this? If she did, Evan did . . . Janis had
said the Tyrell family was one of our best customers. And
Evan was going to marry Alexa Tyrell.

''Did Mars win?''

''Mars's defense system destroyed the enemy ships,
yes.''

''So we won.''

''That depends on one's point of view. All commu-
nication satellites were destroyed. We don't know if other
cities were attacked because Olympia is completely cut off
from the rest of Mars. Here in Olympia we lost every
aircar left on the ground. Our spaceport is closed. If any
of our shuttles remain we can't contact them either. The
subway is closed. Our master computer can't deliver
enough food because warehouse conveyer lines are
jammed. Something's wrong with the water supply. And
no government official is around to take charge. They're
all elites.''

''You're an elite. Why don't you take command of
the city?'' It seemed simple enough.

''No! Risk having the President return and arrest me
for usurping his power? No thank you. My only responsibility is to my cadets.''

''Cadets are alive? I thought—''

''We lost only three.''

I wondered which three but couldn't bear to hear right now. "How did—"

"I ordered them all to go on a field trip to Midtown."

"How did Sergeant Assam die?"

"Three cadets were ill, in the dispensary. She stayed behind with them. She refused to believe me. Her loyalty to the President would not allow her to accept . . ." He shook his head, not finishing the sentence.

"But if you knew Midtown would be safe—"

"I warned her. If she refused to consider her own best interests, that's not my fault."

Her own best interests?

This man who had directed my education, whose authority I'd never questioned, whom I'd always respected, would not meet my gaze. I changed the subject.

"Who assigned Midtown Security to collect and ID casualties? Someone took responsibility there."

"I assume they're doing it because it's the decent thing to do," he said. "After all, many of the dead were elite. Or their staff. They deserve respect."

I glanced over to see if he was being sarcastic. He wasn't. Years of habit made him assume the Midtown Security people felt that much respect for residents of The Fountains.

"Why is there a water shortage, General? In survival training we were taught the reservoirs are buried below all danger. Were the pipes damaged, too?"

"No flooding was reported, but the water pressure is low. I assume it has something to do with the shields being destroyed. Freezing somewhere," he added vaguely.

"Has anybody checked?"

"How should I know?" He looked angry enough to throw me out of the moving car. "That's not my responsibility."

"I thought the academy trained us to 'benefit and protect' not just the President and Council, but all the people of Mars."

General Offrey made an irritating noise, a cross between a sniff and a humph. "My dear young woman," he said, "if you truly believe that, then you should take charge until your father finds the courage to either resign or return. At this point you won't have any competition for the job."

"Because . . ." I was going to say, Because no one would accept me, but that sounded like an excuse. They might accept someone who wanted to help—who was worried about them for a change. At this point they might be glad if *anyone* took charge.

"I do believe that, General. I'm going to do it. Or at least try."

He gave me a startled look. "You can't be serious?"

"Why not? Someone has to do something. You told us long ago we owe a debt to society. Maybe it's time I paid up."

He thought it over and then said grudgingly, "Some might accept you . . . And even if they hate your father, others will be afraid not to accept you. They will assume *he* appointed you—and he might return at any time. No one would think you had the gall to take charge on your own."

The car had come to a stop in the underground lobby of the Midtown Federal Building. Three of the academy's landcars and their ATVs were parked there. Bedraggled people sat on the curb or lay against the walls. Four cadets armed with hi-impact stunners stood guard by the elevator door.

"However, what you're proposing puts me in jeopardy by association," the general went on. "I came to pick you up, not because of your father, but because you're still one of my cadets."

He looked so nervous that I nearly smiled. "General, you know that if something isn't done soon, people will riot for food and water," I said. "Then Midtown will be in jeopardy. If you want to help the cadets, help me."

"Helping you could be worth my life."

"So could not helping me. At least if you help, you won't die feeling ashamed of yourself."

He was still for so long that two of the cadets approached the car to see what was wrong. He waved them away. "What do you want me to do?" he said finally.

WITH HECTOR ON THE SEAT beside me, the ATV cleared the airlock, rolled up the ramp and out onto the main boulevard of the Fountain House complex. In spite of the path that Security had plowed, the treads bumped and crunched over debris.

It was so strange to see embassies and villas—all of

the buildings—standing out there in the open, exposed to the cold, dry twilight of daytime on Mars.

Here and there across the open spaces I could see moving headlights of other vehicles, Security cars collecting the dead.

All the streetlights—those that hadn't broken—were lighted. In the parks and lawns the trees and shrubs were frozen to a frail, brittle blackness. Black grass poked up through the heavy coat of crystal pebbles. Grotesque formations of dirty ice covered the fountains and filled the reflecting pools. The buildings—windows missing, the walls blackened by laser fire—increased my growing sense of dread. Almost every building had a river of dirty ice bulging out the door.

My first stop was the academy. My reason for going there was simple; I needed my civilian clothing.

Going up to the door, Hector walked around the ice where he could and carefully hopped over what couldn't be avoided. I had to watch my footing.

Walking through the familiar lobby wearing a pressure suit felt no more odd than tiptoeing over ice when the gauge on my wrist said the temperature inside the building was forty-three degrees Fahrenheit.

Suddenly I understood the reason for so much ice— the computer system didn't know the shields were gone. It hadn't shut off the heat or water! Without the shields, nighttime temperatures dropped to normal surface levels, minus a hundred degrees Fahrenheit. Pipes froze and burst. As the daytime temperature rose, the heating system melted the ice in the pipes and more water flowed.

If it was the same in all the exposed buildings, that would explain the low water pressures and shortage.

"We have to find who's in charge of utilities, Hector, and have everything shut off out here."

"Noted," said Hector.

Every door in the building was open, forced back by the ice flow. The rooms had been ransacked, drawers dumped, belongings strewn about. Looking around, I wondered if the looting occurred before or after the shield fell.

I had no special feeling for my room at the academy. Unlike the apartment Shala and I had shared in the Sanctuary, the academy was never "home." But I hated to see it trashed and the floor slick with slush. In the sanit the toilet pipe had burst away from the wall. Enough water was running to create a ground fog.

I looted a duffel bag from Evan's room and collected all my clothing I could salvage, including uniforms. Clothes of any kind might soon be in short supply. Every personal keepsake had been taken or destroyed. My guitar was gone, and my three antique books. The books were valuable, but it was losing the guitar that hurt; that had been Shala's gift.

On my way out I saw the food dispensers in the dining room were still full, and so was the automated stockroom behind them. Hector made a note to have the food collected from every building out here.

If it wasn't spoiled by freezing, the kitchen inventory in the hotels and Fountain House alone—not to mention the private residences and embassies—could probably feed most of Midtown for a month. Or at least until we got the food transport tunnels to Midtown open and running again.

From the academy I drove over to Fountain House and stopped in the circular front driveway. The roof was gone, the windows blown out, the building a total ruin. One of the ornate gold entrance doors was missing; the other hung askew. A blue cleaner drone lay in the drive, the only touch of color left.

Tangled under the shrubs near the car was what looked like a long piece of cloth-covered board. Studying it, puzzled by the odd shape, I suddenly realized it was a body that Security had missed. I should have picked it up but did not, telling myself there was no urgency now.

I was going to go inside but lacked the courage. Instead, I circled past the Sanctuary, which had two outer walls missing, and spent the next hour touring the hotels and the spaceport. It was all very depressing, except for one thing.

When I returned from the spaceport to the airlock leading back to Midtown, my headlights glinted over the jagged base of all that remained of The Fountains' crystal shield. I stopped and got out to see how far down the sonar damage went.

What had glinted in the lights was a tough transparent rind covering the crystal base. Under that rind the geometric edges of new crystals were visible.

Like living things too small to see, the nanorobots were at work, rebuilding the shield.

18

OLYMPIA'S STATE BROADCAST STUDIOS WERE ON the top floor of the Federal building. According to plan, General Offrey went there with me. I was afraid I'd be arrested if I just walked in and asked for airtime.

While he spoke with the manager, I studied the wall of control screens. A no-grav fantasy ballet was playing silently on one bank of screens; a casualty list ran on others.

The station was automated, but people were in the control room now, apparently updating the casualty list. Lines kept changing as new names were inserted. Without warning all the screens went to blue.

"Cut to her now?" a man in the control room asked. "OK." He pointed to me, then to a white square on the floor. "You want to stand there, Commander Court?"

Not sure what he had in mind, I moved over to the white square. Before there was time to panic, there I was, on twenty-eight control screens, still dressed in a dusty pressure suit, my face smudged, my hair wild from pulling a helmet on and off.

I turned, located the cameras with visible relief, and then realized I wasn't sure what I should or shouldn't say. Staring at the waiting camera, I decided the best approach was to be honest, to tell the truth, and hope people responded. Taking a deep breath, I began.

"I'm Annalyn Court, one of the President's daughters. He's . . . apparently out of town. So is the Council. I hope the President is monitoring this channel so he'll know he's needed here. But in his absence—and because no one else will do so—I'm taking charge of the city. Someone has to.

"Communications with the outside are cut off. We can't call for help. For all we know, the rest of Mars was as hard hit as Olympia. We're on our own. We have to help ourselves. I'm here to tell you we will survive, if we all work together."

I told them about my drive out to The Fountains and what I'd seen, and about the nanorobots, already rebuilding the shields. About needing to turn off the heat and water out there, and how much food there was—food we could collect and bring back to Midtown.

I asked anyone who knew about utilities, or could work in pressure suits, or had a landcar or ATV, to meet me in the Civic Center auditorium within the hour.

I thanked the medical, security, and broadcast people for the excellent jobs they were doing.

I promised that the homeless, which included me, would have better sanitation facilities and living quarters as soon as we could get more water. And I thanked them for listening and promised to keep them up-to-date on what we were doing and how they could help.

When the cameras went off, the station manager and the people in the control room applauded, but General

Offrey just shook his head and said, "If the President *was* listening, you're in trouble."

Before going to the Civic Center, I stopped at the office General Offrey had found for me. I needed to clean up. There was a shower in the executive sanit. Seeing it made me itch to bathe, but I was ashamed to use so much water. I made do by washing in the sink, brushing my teeth, putting on clean clothes, and brushing the tunnel dust from my hair.

Without the dirt my face still looked strange in the mirror—older, with blue circles under my eyes.

As I was leaving I remembered the bristly little boomerang from that dead man's head was still in a pocket of my dirty uniform. Retrieving it, I poked the thing through the grill of the cold air vent in the sanit for safekeeping.

When he saw me the general was appalled. "Why are you wearing a uniform? Do you want to be shot?"

"They know who I am, General. If I don't respect myself, why should they? Besides, Hector will protect me."

"You're putting all your faith in a robot?"

"He seems to be the only thing available, General."

Being trained to protect the President had some practical benefits. In driving him around the city, we used President's Way, a private transport tunnel linking Fountain House with all the major buildings. I used that route to reach the subbasement of the Civic Center auditorium, and used his security code to take his private elevator up to the stage.

Leaving Hector in the wings where he had a clear

shot at the audience, I walked onstage. The auditorium was crowded and noisy until I appeared; then it went deathly still. A loud, mocking whistle split the silence, setting off boos, catcalls, and, eventually, scattered pleas for "quiet!"

There was a lectern at stage center. Reaching it, I placed my hands on either side of its desktop, hoping to look confident, but in fact needing to hold on because my knees were shaking.

"Thank you for coming."

The lectern's PA controls were set too low for the noise. Turning up the volume, I repeated, "Thank you for coming." The crowd quieted.

"Where's your father?" an angry woman called.

"I don't know." That was true, and I didn't know where the President was either.

"If you're taking charge of the city, where were you the last two days?" a man shouted.

"In the MedCen."

"What makes you think you can do the job?"

"What makes you think I can't?"

"Do we have to kneel to you?" another man called out.

"No!"

"Good!" That shout was greeted with enthusiastic applause.

There was a sudden commotion at the rear of the room. Heads turned and boos greeted General Offrey as he came in, leading the cadets. All were in uniform. They formed a line along the rear wall, a standing border of green and gold.

I turned the volume way up to say, "Thank you for coming, General Offrey." The sound was so loud people jumped, and the booing stopped. My point was made: they couldn't outshout me. In the lull I added, "Midtown needs your help."

"Is that why you brought the military and a protector robot with you?" the same angry woman called. "To help *us?*"

"If you were me, would you have the nerve to stand up here alone?" I asked her.

"No . . . ," she admitted, and when I grinned at her honesty, she actually laughed, and part of the crowd laughed, too. The worst of the tension evaporated. And I made a mental note about the power of laughter.

"General Offrey and the cadets came because they want to help," I explained. "Cadets are trained in handling emergency situations. As for my robot, his name is Hector. My mother gave him to me—and I'm very grateful she did. He kept me alive these past few days. And yes, I brought him along because I was afraid. But if you want me to, I'll command him to shut off."

There was some discussion among the crowd before a man called out: "Forget the robot. We're not going to harm her and he's not going to hurt us. We're wasting time. Let's get started."

Slowly the big room quieted until the only sounds were a few coughs.

"First things first," I began. "Does anyone here know how to turn off the water to the exposed complexes?"

"Yes!"

Three voices answered, and I knew the meeting was going to work. "Can you do it today?"

"Yes!"

Hector recorded their names on my command.

"Can the heat be shut off out there?"

"We can turn it off grid by grid," a man called. "The spaceport's a separate system. That'll take longer."

"The heat traces on the pipes—they keep the water from freezing under normal conditions—will go off when we shut off the power," another man explained. "But before we turn them off, we should pump as much of that water as we can back into Midtown's reservoir."

The meeting worked! And General Offrey turned out to be as capable an administrator as he was a commandant. With his help I set up the various work crews we needed and had Hector devise a priority system to handle basic emergencies first.

Once we got down to details, there was a lot of enthusiasm and remarkably little friction. People seemed glad to be able to do something constructive. Crew leaders, chosen for their expertise, formed their own council, selected their teams, and went to work.

Some jobs seemed impossible—like figuring out how to get into a sealed conveyor system to clean out a jam-up of spoiled and stinking food—but our successes were sweet.

Within a week, Midtown's residents had returned to a safe and sanitary—if not normal—life.

The refugees' lives improved too. Restaurant owners volunteered to take charge of feeding them. With the help of some of Shala's friends and customers, I had Shala's Place converted into a dining room but couldn't bring myself to go see it.

When our full water supply was restored, temporary sanits were set up and connected to the recycling system. Some of us had our first shower since the attack. It was wonderful. Sonar cleaners were set up in public places so clothing could be cleaned, free of charge. The air began to smell better.

We tried to keep all the refugees, who could and would, busy helping others; they had the most reason to grieve and needed the least time to brood.

Over eight thousand people died when the shields collapsed. Working with Security and medical personnel, General Offrey and the cadets helped dispose of the bodies. For residents the law was clear: cremation. But the hotel victims included tourists and business travelers from across Mars and a hundred off-world cities. After being identified, they were placed in temporary morgues until their next of kin could be notified.

Without Hector my job would have been so much harder. He kept track of progress, reminding me daily of what had to be done next. He did everything from talking to the computers that kept Midtown running, to finding the schematic that allowed the engineers to link the shelters to the recycle system, to searching census files for people we needed with special training, from obscure languages to artistic talents.

Out of his "special talents" search came a dozen different projects, many of them for the aid of traumatized children.

Going everywhere with me, Hector became a celebrity—to the point that people would yell "Hey, Hector!" from across the street, often before they greeted me. *If* they greeted me first, it was usually because they had a problem they wanted solved. And I was proud they felt free enough to act that way.

There wasn't time to worry about protocol or anything except what had to be done next. After living such a sheltered life, and being taught that being elite made us superior to all others, I learned during those hectic days that I'd been misinformed. I liked these Midtown people, and I wished for their sake that the President would never come back.

Odd as it may seem, for the first time in my life there were moments when I was aware of being happy. It was *fun* being in charge, dashing around, making decisions, solving problems, even getting blisters shoveling sand— we all shoveled sand.

I woke up looking forward to each day and fell asleep at night exhausted, oblivious to the hardness of my office floor.

At last we got the spoiled food cleaned out of the tunnels, got the conveyors repaired and running smoothly so that the auto-serve in everyone's apartment could be used again. When that was announced on the news, people cheered me in the streets. For the next few hours I went around with a silly grin on my face.

As the last of the homeless moved up out of Central Station and into temporary shelters set up in the parks and plazas, we began the biggest job—repairing the subway tunnels.

The worst was over. Or the best. For then I had time to think.

19

WHEN I WASN'T SO TIRED, SLEEP BECAME A PROB-
lem. Bad dreams woke me. Alone in the office—I slept
on the floor for lack of beds—I'd think about Shala and
cry. The tears were for myself as much as for her. Without
her I felt completely alone, orphaned.

Sometimes self-doubt would overwhelm me. What
did I think I was doing? Should I do more? Were people
satisfied with the way things were going—or were they
afraid to say?

What if, when we got the subways running again and
could get to the other cities, everybody there was dead?

I worried about Evan. Was he safe? Regardless of
what he had or hadn't done, I still loved him. But lately
I wasn't sure I liked him. And I didn't trust him anymore.
Was that unfair of me? He had to follow the President's
orders, to say nothing of his mother's.

Where was the President? Could he monitor our
broadcasts? Did he know what I was doing? If he
came back, how long would it be before he tried to kill
me?

Could he come back? The invading mercenaries had
been destroyed but not the rebels here in Midtown. De-
pending on their strength, he might need an army. Which

would mean more fighting, more deaths. Was there any way to prevent that?

To escape from all these morbid thoughts I'd get dressed again and go out for a walk in the Greenway—the park that stretches from central Midtown to the zoo and botanical garden.

Hector's feet made soft raking sounds in the gravel on the serpentine paths. With the water supply back to normal, the misters ran all night. The smells of wet lawns, herbs, and roses were soothing.

Late at night the Greenway was so quiet you could hear the lions coughing from a long way off. I often went all the way down to the botanical garden. There by the little lake the trees blocked the city lights and the stars were visible over the crater rim. I'd sit on a park bench and look out.

With its shield gone, the Imaji Hotel was a cluster of pale gold geometrics faintly visible in the reflected light from Midtown. The pagoda roof of the Buddhist temple looked like black pearl and the ice was a dull pink from dust. No matter how often I searched the sky for the moving lights of a shuttle or a spaceship, I saw none.

On the plaza in front of the Federal Building, as on plazas all over Midtown, a village of bubble tents housed the homeless. No matter how late I came back, people were awake.

Maybe they had bad dreams too and were tired of thinking and crying, or trying to sleep with their lights on. Instead, they made the dining areas into impromptu outdoor cafés, sitting there sipping drinks and talking.

One night I passed a tent where people were talking inside and overheard a woman say, "It's a pity Court's not our President. She works hard, she got things running well again, and she seems to care. Can you imagine *him* helping *us?*"

I stopped to listen.

"Maybe we're rid of him," a man answered. "Maybe those stupid speeches of his broadcast right after the attack were old tapes. Maybe he was killed that day and they're afraid to say so."

"If they know," the first speaker said.

Another woman said, "It would be nice if all of them from Fountain House died, but that's too much to hope for."

There was a ripple of appreciative laughter and then a man said, "Did you know he was president when my grandmother was a girl? She was a hundred and fifteen when she died last year."

The voices became inaudible until a woman said, "That's what they say—him and the whole Council. I believe it."

"If it's true, there's nothing in the Constitution that says we have to accept that. That's being governed by robots," the man said. "We should demand an election. I'd campaign for Court."

"We could replace the Council with some of the Recovery team people. That Ituro Menendez, who fixed the water supply; he's smart. And Kami Ivanov, she's smart, too, and . . ."

It occurred to me that I was eavesdropping on treason. I tiptoed away.

A sandstorm started later that same night.

Without our weather satellites to warn us, the fact that the storm struck at night, when everyone was still safe inside the shield, saved lives—to say nothing of equipment we couldn't afford to lose.

Because I grew up in Fountain House, in the most sheltered part in the crater, sandstorms had never frightened me. But this one did; the winds blasted and howled and screamed against the Midtown shield.

Either the storm was especially bad, or the missing shields gave it more room to play inside the crater. The wind seemed merciless, unceasingly driving dense sand and gravel against the shield, enclosing us inside in our unease. People stood in the streets, staring up at the roof, afraid it would break.

Flamelike, eerie yellow-orange lightning would build on the leeward side of the shield, beneath the overblowing sand. At times, something—perhaps friction or minerals in the sand—caused blue, green, or purple balls of light like Saint Elmo's fire, which would dissipate with loud popping noises.

Green ball lightning formed inside the shield, dancing beneath the roof or floating down to street level, where it sped along almost purposefully, seeming to chase screaming people before disappearing as mysteriously as it came.

Between the lightning and noise of the storm, many

people living in the bubble tents grew so afraid that they moved back down into the station and tunnels again.

That wind could break the massive shield seemed unthinkable, but sound had destroyed the other shields and, with them, our faith in our own invulnerability.

Still, we could either sit and worry, or get on with repairing the subway system. That project was going slowly.

While exploring the underground roadways before the storm hit, we'd found the subway maintenance shop out by the spaceport. In that shop was a work train. Everyone was elated. We thought we could take that work train out to the Midtown Central Station, and on to Wind Canyon, reopen that station, and go on to Regis, the nearest city.

Then we discovered the subway tunnel to the maintenance shop had been closed off by explosive charges so massive that much of the surrounding bedrock had caved in or was threatening to collapse.

Whoever was in charge of sealing off the city had done a thorough job. The more I saw of these bombed tunnels the more I thought of the President calling Midtowners "traitors" and wondered if he'd decided that if he was attacked, it would be their fault . . . and he'd had Midtown sealed in to die.

Once we located the equipment we needed, it took three weeks of hazardous, hard, round-the-clock work to get that tunnel dug out and reopened and the repair train out onto the main line. It's been a long time since Martians have had to do manual labor—we've lost the knack, as well as the muscles.

They wouldn't let me help. The third day on the job one of the women took me aside and said, "Please don't be insulted, Commander Court, but I've been elected to tell you we don't want you working out here. If you get hurt by a cave-in, who'll be in charge of the city?"

"But this is the most important job we have to do—"

"We decided you can help by setting up a system for food and water on the site. Get some portable sanits moved into the maintenance shop—things like that."

The President would have killed anyone who decided he could provide portable sanits, but I did what they asked. It was just as useful, if not half as much fun.

The last step was to move the trains sitting in Central Station onto side rails so our work train could get through.

At four the next morning Security called me. "Great news!" The woman's voice was loud with excitement. "The subway's open! A work train from Regis just pulled into Central Station! And they've repaired the communications cable in the tunnels. We can talk with the rest of the world again!"

Groggy as I was, it was almost too much to take in all at once. "That's wonderful!" I managed to say.

"There's about fifty people here, Commander, and they're hungry. They've been working nonstop to get here."

"Bring them over to the Federal Building for breakfast."

After calling General Offrey and asking him to call the leaders of our Recovery teams, I called the broadcast station so all of Midtown would wake up to the good news.

I was in the sanit washing my face with cold water to wake up when the personal meaning of the news hit me: it was only a matter of time until the President had to return!

20

THE BUILDING WAS SILENT WITH SLEEP. IN THE empty dining room I checked the food servers to make sure they were full. I knew they would be, but occupying myself kept me from thinking: the President's going to kill me.

Waiting, I watched the screens that covered the window wall during a storm. They were showing lush green landscapes dotted with woolly animals in a place called Scotland. In the background, Earth's clear blue sky made me want to go there. It seemed so clean and gentle, so safe compared to Mars. Then I thought of the President's "river room" and shivered.

A murmur of conversation in the hall announced General Offrey and a large group of strangers. As they hurried in, their excited voices faded to whispers; they slowed and stopped to look around and gradually fell silent, perhaps feeling out of place in the elegant room in their grimy coveralls.

"Commander Court," the general said as he came over to me, "may I present our rescuers from Regis. Ladies and gentlemen . . ."

He paused, as surprised as I was to see the Regians dropping to their knees, assuming the Attitude of Respect.

"Please, don't do that," I told the group. No one moved. "On your feet! Now!" My anger showed in my voice, which is probably why they got up. But I wasn't angry at them; I was mad at the *man* who made them do this humiliating thing.

By the time I'd shaken hands and thanked each of them, either my manner or their hunger had relaxed them enough so that some headed off to the food dispensers while others went to the sanits to wash up.

"How badly was your city damaged by the attack?" I asked their chief engineer, a woman perhaps ten years older than I.

"We weren't attacked," she said. "No other city was."

"At the risk of sounding ungrateful, why didn't anyone fly over to Olympia before this sandstorm began?"

"We didn't know you were attacked until we got here—they told us in the station. I'm still not sure what happened—"

"Did you lose satellite transmission?"

"Yes."

"Didn't that worry anyone? Didn't they think to try to contact the capital to find out why? And maybe worry when the cable was out, too, and they couldn't reach us?"

"I suppose they did, but that's not my—"

"Nobody saw the laser lights in the sky?"

"Regis is over a hundred miles away," the general tactfully reminded me, "and we're in the deepest crater."

"No SOS went out from here?"

"If it did, we didn't hear it," she said. "When the satellites died, Regis Control closed our spaceports to all but emergency landings. The computer said there were problems in the subsurface system, and it was attempting to reroute. We assumed it would until—I think it was the next morning—it seems so long ago. Anyhow, we didn't start to worry until we heard the subway to Olympia was closed."

"Yet nobody thought to fly here to check?" I said.

"Without clearance from the weather satellite, no flights are allowed," she reminded me. "The threat of sandstorms—" Her hands began to shake so she spilled her coffee and hurried to set down the cup. Which made me feel like a bully. She was afraid of me, of the power she thought I represented.

"I'm sorry. I'm not blaming you," I said, trying to be reassuring, "but under the circumstances, I think someone should have taken the chance."

Visibly taking a deep breath to calm down, she found her courage. "Probably no one came here because we all—every town had problems of their own. And who would think anyone would dare attack the capital? Or that the defense system would fail? Who let that happen? Where *is* the President?"

"Good questions," I said, "and you aren't the first to ask them. The general and I will explain as much as we know over breakfast. In any case, we are very grateful to you all."

During breakfast we learned the rest of Mars had heard nothing from the President, not even his out-of-date broadcasts. The Regians' questions were discreet, but their curiosity was as understandable as their growing concern for the President's whereabouts.

"Gossip says his wife is in Itek," one of the Regians said, "with her son. They planned to go out to the Greenhouse Habitat, but with the satellites out, no space shuttle could take off. She'll probably come here now as soon as she can."

"Perhaps not. Not when she sees the newscasts," General Offrey said. "The First Lady is used to luxury. And with The Fountains gone and all the luxury hotels closed . . ." He left the obvious unsaid.

"I'd be back here on the first train," the Regian said. "Just to find out if my friends and loved ones were safe."

Yes, but you are a kind, normal person, I thought. I was sure we wouldn't see Janis here until The Fountains was rebuilt and shielded again. I was wrong.

With the underground cable repaired, for the first time since the attack we could broadcast our news to the rest of Mars. Unfortunately this included the news anchor saying that I was "ably in charge in the President's absence."

We in turn learned that seven new satellites had been placed into orbit around Mars. The satellites were the gift of our nearest neighbor in space, the Greenhouse Habitat. The new weather satellites showed the current sandstorm covered half the planet, including all major cities.

Travel was still impossible, but the second work train from Regis arrived the next day. Hector and I were in Central Station with a social services team from the

MedCen. We were trying to convince the people who had moved back there when the storm began to move out again up-level, where they would be just as safe, and out of the way when the station reopened.

The tunnels were being cleaned; train cars had been shunting about all morning. Busy listening to a mother whose small child was terrified by the wind's noise, I didn't even notice the second work train's arrival.

Suddenly a familiar, arrogant voice called, "Annalyn Court! There you are! We must talk! Now!" I turned, saw the new subway car—and Janis walking toward me.

Everyone around fell silent, as shocked by her appearance as I was. It wasn't that she was there; it was how she looked. She was the luxury we had almost forgotten existed.

In the days since the disaster, with so much hard, dirty work to be done, no one had had time to pay much attention to appearance. We had all fallen into the habit of wearing anything that came to hand, so long as it was clean. Now here was Janis, her shining hair perfectly cut and styled, wearing a peach velvet tunic and tights, with belt and boots in a deeper matched shade, and lots of gold jewelry. Her perfumed elegance was almost an insult to our shabbiness.

After excusing myself to the woman and child and leaving them in the care of the social worker, I went to greet Janis and told her, "We can talk in the security office."

"You look terrible," was the first thing she said. Loudly. "And we'll talk right here." She gave a sarcastic laugh. "No wonder you don't want anyone else to hear what I have to say. You know you have no authority to tell me or anyone else what to do. I want people to hear me."

"Don't make a scene, Janis."

"Why not? It's time *someone* made a scene! Who put you in charge? No one! You're a little opportunist, taking advantage of other people's tragedy!"

She had always used anger to intimidate. When I was small I was afraid of her rages. No more. As I watched and listened to her, I just found her tiresome.

"How did you get here, Janis? And why? We don't have room to house you, or the time to cater to you."

"How dare you speak to me like that!"

Her roar of outrage attracted the attention of everyone in the station who hadn't already noticed her—as she intended. Several Security guards came running. Hector's warning lights came on. He moved in front of me to position himself to fire. I made no effort to stop him.

"Shut your mouth, lady!" suggested a man in the crowd gathering around us. "You can't talk that way to Commander Court."

She wheeled on him. "What's your name? We'll see who's in charge here! I'll have you both arrested. Do you know who I am?"

"We know!" A man who'd just told me he'd lost his only child spoke up. "And we know what you are. Go back where you came from!"

Angry shouts of agreement drowned out Janis's reply. I have to hand it to her—she didn't seem fazed at all. But maybe she simply didn't understand the situation.

"Do you need help, Commander?" The Security guards pushed through the crowd to my side.

"Guard, I want her and these other people arrested!" Janis said in her most imperious tones—and I held my breath.

The guards didn't even look at her. "Do you need help, Commander Court?" the senior officer repeated.

"Not if we send the First Lady out to Fountain House!" a man called before I could answer. "Without a pressure suit!"

"And send the rest of her friends after her—if they have the nerve to come back!"

I think it was the crowd's laughter as much as the guards ignoring her that finally got through to Janis; she began to look worried. She had always been held in almost as much awe and fear as the President—although I'm sure she thought of it as "respect." Now the "respect" was clearly gone.

As for me, for the first time I truly began to grasp how much of the President's power had crumbled along with the shield over Fountain House. If he and the Council returned, force and habit might help reinstate them, but they would never again hold the unquestioned power of the past.

And when The Fountains' crystal shield was secure again, it would protect only the buildings beneath it—if the winds hadn't blown everything away.

21

"QUIET!"

The crowd went still at my shout. Noting their response, Janis's eyes narrowed. She gave me a brief, speculative glance, as if reassessing both my situation and her own. Hector and I headed toward the Security office. People moved aside to let us pass.

"I'll get my bag," said Janis, catching up with me. "We'll talk in the VIP lounge."

"We can't. People are living there."

"In the VIP lounge? *Commoners?*"

"Homeless people."

"They can sleep on the streets. It's warm enough."

She made no effort to keep her voice down. People close enough to hear repeated what she said to the others.

I knew she was arrogant. I'd never thought she was stupid until then. Leaning close, I whispered into her jeweled and perfumed ear: "If you don't shut up you're going to start a riot. These people might kill you—with good cause. We'll talk in the Security office."

She jerked away, giving me a look of pure hate, but she quit talking and followed.

A man was standing in the Security office, his back to the door. Dressed in a tight black suit with knee-high black boots, he looked as elegant as Janis. As the door slid open for us he turned.

"Evan! You're safe!"

"Annie." My welcoming hug must have thrown him off balance, because he sort of stumbled back, freeing himself to step awkwardly over their bags on the floor. "I was just asking where you were. I see Mother's solved the problem, as usual."

"Yes, she's . . . remarkable. Come in here." I pulled him after me into one of the interview rooms. Janis and Hector followed.

"What are you doing here, Evan? Is the President with you? Where's your uniform?"

"Hey, slow down," he said, laughing. "I—we just got here."

"Where's the President?"

For a moment he looked irritated, then shrugged. "OK, if it's so important to you. I'm not wearing a uniform because I thought it might be smarter not to. And I don't know where the President is. I haven't seen him since you did."

"But you stayed with him—"

"No. After you left, he decided I should go to Itek for real. He said you'd be there. When you weren't . . ."

"We know where she ran off to, don't we?" Janis cut in, venom in her voice. "And we know why."

That remark was so unfair I lost my temper. "You know nothing, Janis. You—"

"I know you shouldn't be in charge of the capital," she cut in again. "You're obviously no leader. Evan, you should have seen how people behaved to me out there just now. They're completely out of control."

"You're lucky they didn't mob you—"

Ignoring me, she went on talking to Evan. "There's also the unfortunate fact that her being here like this might make people think *she's* his heir . . ." She frowned and turned on me again. "Let me see your orders, Annalyn. I can't believe Charles sent you here without telling me."

"Why don't you ask him?" I sounded as cold and confident as she did, which made her hesitate.

"Yes . . . I will."

"You know where he's hiding?"

"He's not *hiding!* Is that what you've told these commoners?" Before I could answer, she went on. "As in any emergency, the federal government moved to a deep-shelter suite for the duration. After all, there's no secure place fit for him to stay in Midtown."

"That's not true. He could stay—"

Giving me a look that said he thought I was naive, Evan interrupted to ask his mother, "How long do you think he'll stay down there?" Unlike me, he seemed to know what a deep-shelter suite was.

"As long as he likes," said Janis. "The pioneers lived there for years—until the domes were complete. Charles had several suites modernized. For security reasons he may decide to stay until Fountain House is rebuilt."

"So he's somewhere under this crater?" I asked, thinking that made sense. Why else would she have come back here? And wouldn't she have told Evan her plans? Why was he talking like this was all new to him?

"Why don't you call the President? Use that phone."

Janis ignored my suggestion. "Evan, I want you to take charge of Midtown. Discipline and order must be restored before things get out of hand. Order Security to enforce the rules, with guns if necessary. I know your father would approve that."

For a moment Evan said nothing. I assumed he was trying to think of a tactful way to refuse—to make her understand there was no way he could go out there and do this. But then he turned to me and said, "Mother's right, Annie. Sorry. I'm taking over now."

Anger, disappointment, and sadness all made a painful knot form in my chest, but there wasn't time for any of it. I stepped back to put Hector between myself and my enemies.

"Prepare to stun them if they move, Hector."

"Armed," said Hector.

"Annie? What are you doing?"

"Don't move. A stun is quite painful."

Janis glanced from me to Hector's warning lights and for the first time doubt flickered in her eyes.

"Annie—you can't be serious?" Evan's face was pale. "It's nothing personal, Annie. I mean, we'd let you stay here in Olympia. It's not like I'd sentence you to exposure or anything. You—"

"You and your mother have no authority here. If you try again to interfere, both of you will be arrested and detained. Is that understood?"

"I'd say she sounds like she's in control." Evan managed to give me one of his most charming smiles.

"She has no authority over us!"

"I do so long as you're in Midtown, Janis," I said quietly. "You can stay here peacefully if you can find housing, or you can go back where you came from—or go find the President. But I will not allow you to create more problems. Is that clear?"

"It's clear you'll die when the President hears about this!" She glared at me as if believing sheer will would intimidate me. I held her gaze until she looked away.

"Am I allowed to leave without getting shot?" she said then. "I can't stand being in the same room with you!"

"Annie, please? Call off Hector. You know Mother. She sometimes speaks without thinking."

"Then she'd better start thinking. There aren't enough Security guards to protect her if she starts a riot."

"I want out of this room. Now!" snapped Janis.

"Hector. Weapons check."

"Done. One weapon in her right boot. One weapon in each of his boots. Do you wish them to disarm?"

"Yes."

"No! We must be able to protect ourselves!"

"Annie, you—"

"You first, Evan. Slowly." I'd taken my gun from its hiding place in my belt. "Remember the routine from class. Put them on the floor and step back. Good. Now Janis."

Between them they were carrying a pair of the slim

laser pistols we called assassinators; Evan's other weapon was what I think is a lal gun. I was afraid to examine it.

After sweeping the weapons aside with my foot, I said, "Hector, Janis Parker is allowed to leave the room."

As the door closed behind her, Evan said, "You wouldn't really arrest us, would you?"

"Yes."

His smile faded. "You wouldn't dare."

"It's not a matter of daring, Evan. I'll do anything necessary to keep the peace. You don't seem to understand the situation. People are angry, disgusted with the President and the whole elite class. Eight thousand people died here. Did you know that? Do you care?"

"Sure," he said. "But what good would it have done for us to stay and die, too?" He was looking through the glass door at Janis. "Besides, they can afford to rebuild. It's not like anyone in The Fountains was poor."

"Oh, Evan!" I said, disgusted. "Why don't you step outside and say that? Tell it to Shala's ghost, and Sergeant Assam's, and all the thousands of others who were killed, including three of our classmates."

There was a long, angry silence. Finally he said, "I'm sorry about Shala. She was always nice to me. And I'm sorry about what Mother said. As soon as we heard about you . . . she insisted on coming here. You know how impossible she is."

"Don't try to blame it all on Janis. You knew why she wanted to come—to get rid of me. In fact, I wouldn't be surprised if that wasn't your idea. You're trying to hide behind her, just like you did when we were little."

For a moment I thought he was going to hit me. He might have tried if Hector hadn't spoken: "Relax your arm. Step back. This is your only warning."

"Shut up, Hector," Evan said but obeyed, adding, "you're not up to this, Annie. Not without Hector. So don't let a little power go to your head."

"Even if that were true, you want that 'little power,' don't you?"

"Yes." He looked straight at me. "So what do *you* know, Annie? What did you learn out there on the *Capri* that you could blackmail the President with? Because as I see it, blackmail's the only explanation for why you're in charge here and not me." And he smiled.

I couldn't believe he'd said that, or that I could feel such contempt for him.

"I'm here because I followed orders. When things didn't turn out the way I expected, I did the best I could—just as we were taught."

His smile died. "Come on, Annie. Even you can't expect me to believe that."

"What you believe doesn't matter to me anymore. Hector, show him out."

After he was gone I sat down, exhausted and sick at heart. It seemed everything that once had mattered was over or ending.

What would happen if they found the President? If he was hiding somewhere under the crater, then surely he or his staff monitored our news broadcasts. He must know where I was and what I was doing. All he had to do to stop me was come back.

And when he did? Now that the trains were running again, should I leave while I could? But what would happen to the people here?

I jumped when the door opened. "Sorry to startle you, Commander," the officer apologized. "The First Lady's at the front desk. She wants—she demands a landcar. I told her they're all in use. She's getting nasty."

"Take mine. Make sure the tracking unit is on and monitor her route like you do when I drive. And print it."

"Do you know where she wants to go?"

"To find the President."

"Where is he?"

I grinned. "Maybe we'll find out?"

Later that day Security reported Janis went first to deep vaults under the Sanctuary where a still-functioning camera showed her and Evan loading oxygen canisters into the car. Neither Security nor I knew those vaults existed.

From there they used an airlock and freight elevator so unknown that the computer brought up a map from archives to show it. That map was so old it showed the original single dome over Olympia as "under construction."

They took that elevator down to sublevel six. We'd never known there was a sublevel six. Our deepest factories and the reservoirs were on sublevel five. An even older map came on-screen then, Security said, and the blinking *X* representing Janis's car crossed that map—and disappeared.

"I heard there's a ghost city down there somewhere," the Security captain said. "Cramped rooms, long halls, enough atmosphere to make things white with frost. I always thought it was just a scary story for kids."

"Did you get print copies of the old maps?"

"Yes. Do we have to go after them?" The captain didn't sound enthusiastic. "Is that where the old—uh, sorry—the President is hiding?"

"She thinks so," I said. "And no, we won't go after them."

22

BY LATE EVENING ALL THE HOMELESS HAD BEEN moved out of Central Station. Again. The subway cars were clean; the tunnels soon would be. Drones were polishing the floors. Everything smelled of wax and disinfectant.

I left with the cadet crew. It felt good to have accomplished so much, but most of us were too tired to enjoy it. When Hector passed us on the up ramp, I envied him his power cell. He never got tired—but then he probably never felt a sense of satisfaction either.

It was dinnertime; the streets were nearly deserted. At the Federal Building the cadets went inside for dinner. Too tired to eat, I excused myself and went over to sit on the stone bench that circled the plaza fountain.

Across the way the café tables were crowded. People were talking and laughing, but I couldn't hear them for the wind outside and the splashing water behind me. Which was nice. Just sitting quietly after talking with people all day was a luxury.

I thought of calling Security again to ask if Janis and Evan had come back on the map, then decided Captain Capra, the Security chief, would have called me if they had any news.

Leaning back, I watched the Saint Elmo's fire up under the roof peaks. Globules of green light were moving with fluid grace, flowing into amoebic shapes, breaking into balls, drifting in an unseen current. Watching them was soothing.

I had nearly dozed off when my communicator beeped. A voice said, "Commander? Captain Capra here. We're picking up an odd, intermittent signal you might want to see."

"What kind of signal?"

"Uh . . . it looks like a ghost car, racing through tunnels that don't exist. It came on-screen way out beyond Fountain House and looks like it's headed for Midtown."

His words took my breath away like a punch in the stomach. It wasn't that I didn't expect something like this, but not so soon. Without time to run. Or a place to run to. I took a deep breath and exhaled slowly.

"Commander?"

"Yes. There are tunnels only the President uses."

"Secret tunnels?"

"Yes. He might be coming back with—"

"You want us to arrest them if they surface?"

"For their protection?"

"For yours. For all of us. I'll tell you, Commander, nobody is going to brush dust again. Not for anyone."

"Brush dust" was what people now called the Attitude of Respect.

"You're talking treason, Captain."

"I'm talking truth."

I stopped listening. Thick curtains of dust had begun to jet up along the front of the Federal Building. My first thought was that airlocks had failed somewhere and the storm was forcing its way inside. Between Capra's news and this, adrenaline erased my fatigue.

"Capra, check the airlocks! There's dust shooting up from the pavement here in Federal Plaza!"

"Danger!" Hector warned. "Danger! Take cover."

"Commander? What's going on?"

"Check the airlocks!"

"They're secure. What's happen—?" A blast of static drowned him out.

Wide cracks split the pavement. I moved halfway around the fountain. Diners at the café stood to see what was going on. A great oblong slab began to raise like a trapdoor, powered by massive hydraulic lifts on either side.

Light from below turned the dust into haze and cast moving shadows on the under slab. One shadow moved ahead, assumed human shape, and became a silhouette.

"It *is* the President!" I whispered to my communicator, and heard Captain Capra swear. "He's coming up . . . what looks like an escalator buried under the plaza —Hector, get over here!"

"Hide!" the captain ordered. "Help's on the way!"

No matter how good it sounded, I was too proud to be seen running away.

Before the slab was fully raised, six shadows became guards bounding up the moving steps past the President to fan out onto the plaza. Each dropped to a defensive crouch, guns threatening the crowd. Their assault lasers could melt shield walls.

The President himself came into view, immaculate in gold and white. Stepping off the escalator he stopped, slowly turned to look at the buildings, nodded as if pleased to see they were intact, and then watched the Saint Elmo's fire . . . like a tourist taking in the sights.

Colonel Haddad, riding up the escalator behind him, had no room to step off. When she stumbled into him, he moved just enough for her to get by.

Next up came Janis and Evan to take their places beside him. Neither seemed surprised at where they were. Both wore pressure suits but carried their helmets. They couldn't have gone out on the surface in the storm— which meant they'd found him in a place without adequate atmosphere for living humans.

While all this was going on, people were filling the balconies and walkways connecting some of the residential buildings around the plaza. Seeing the President, a few dropped to their knees; others darted back into their apartments.

Most watched, standing in silence. Maybe because that's what I was doing. I wasn't going to kneel and I couldn't think of what to say to him. Then he saw me and solved the problem.

"Arrest Commander Court." He pointed. Colonel Haddad started toward me.

"Halt," Hector warned. Haddad slowed to glance back at the President for further instructions.

"Don't touch her!" someone yelled from a balcony.

"Keep away from her or you'll be sorry!" another called.

Two guards aimed up at the balconies, provoking outraged yells from all over. The other four guards jumped to their feet, backing toward the President to give him maximum coverage, nervously turning from side to side. Colonel Haddad also backed toward him, obviously worried about the threat of the crowd.

"Do you believe me now?" Evan was speaking to the President but his voice carried. "Your favorite's a traitor!"

"Evan!"

"Drop the innocent act, Annie," he warned. "If it wasn't for you, they'd all be kneeling."

That remark seemed to make the President aware of the crowd for the first time. Frowning, he turned to Colonel Hadded. "What's going on here? Get them on their knees! NOW! ON YOUR KNEES, ALL OF YOU!"

His voice rose to such a chilling roar that a few people instantly obeyed out of fear. I was fascinated, wondering what sort of amplifiers were built into him. His show of anger had the opposite effect from what he expected.

"We won't kneel!" a voice rang out. "Never again!"

"What respect did you show us?"

"You didn't care if we all died."

"You're going to need an army to threaten us!"

"Go back where you came from!"

There was a loud boo. Others joined in. The booing spread, almost drowning out the sandstorm.

"Ten seconds, then fire into the crowd," I heard the President order his guards.

"Stop it!" Jumping up onto the bench I waved my arms to get their attention. "Quiet! Quiet!"

When I could be heard, I called to him: "If you kill us for not kneeling, how do you explain that to the rest of Mars? How will you justify it? Everyone knows what happened here."

"I don't have to explain anything," he said. "Not to you or anyone. I'm the President."

Hearing sirens whooping toward the plaza, he told his guards, "When Security gets here we'll take three of their cars. Commander Court will come with me. Destroy the robot."

"No!" I jumped down in front of Hector.

"Hold it." Brushing past the guards, the President came toward me. "Annalyn." His voice was soft, almost seductive. "What have you been doing? I trusted you. And you do this?"

"If you trusted me," I said, sounding braver than I felt, "why did you try to kill me?"

"I sent you to Itek—to safety."

"You sent me to the Wind Canyon station to die. And I would have died if I hadn't dug my way out and walked to Midtown."

He frowned, studying my face, then looked at Colonel Haddad.

The colonel was about to speak when Evan said, "How she got here doesn't matter, sir. What matters is she's assumed your authority. She's turned the capital against you. You can't pretend she hasn't."

The President hesitated, then agreed with what sounded like regret. "He's right, Annalyn. I can't forgive treason. Now step aside."

Hector tried to edge past me; I moved with him.

"Step aside, Annalyn!" The President took his gun from its holster.

As if that were a signal, laser fire burst from every balcony and walkway above the Plaza. The guards fell; four lay still, two others writhed in pain.

Janis hit the ground and rolled, Evan right behind her. Calling something to her, he rolled to the far end of the opening in the pavement and swung his legs over. After clinging there for a second, white-knuckled, he dropped from sight. Janis followed and, with a wonderful backflip, so did Colonel Haddad.

The President sank slowly to his knees. The yelling and the laser fire stopped. I could hear the storm again, and the fountain. I didn't even look to see if I was hit. I just stood there stupidly wondering: where did people get the weapons?

The lull ended with people bursting from a side street, yelling and screaming. My first thought was that the President had more guards who were chasing them. Then I saw they were running away from a big, meandering glob of ball lightning.

The noise seemed to rouse the President. Still gripping his gun, he used his hands to push himself to his feet. Once erect, he staggered in a circle. When his back was to me, I saw three black, smoking holes in his white uniform.

Regaining some control, he turned around again, looking as if he was trying to remember why he was here. Our eyes met, and I knew he was going to kill me.

"I'm sorry, Annalyn."

When he raised his gun, it was my turn to hit the pavement and roll. Grit cut into my hands and knees.

Hector fired first. His laser power would have fried an ordinary person. But after taking four more direct hits, the President was still able to shoot Hector and then me before renewed firing from the balconies hit him. Even after he fell, his finger clutched the trigger. The beam of his gun blazed against the fountain's base until I could smell melting stone.

I remember thinking: *So this is how it feels to be shot. They say there isn't any pain. They lie.*

At the same time another part of my mind was glad Hector felt nothing. Part of him was melted, black and gooey. A few of his lights flashed weakly.

As if attracted by the laser fire, the ball lightning quit meandering and raced toward us. It looked so cool and green that I wanted it to cover me, to take away the burning. I was disappointed when it chose the President instead.

It engulfed him like a cloud. One moment he was glowing inside that green cloud and then something sparked—and he and the lightning exploded.

Hector and I were lifted and thrown back. Pieces of

the android flew like shrapnel. There were cries and wails.

One of the last things I remember, and wish I could forget, was the smell, like a sickly sweet electrical fire.

By gripping the rim of a tree planter, I managed to pull myself to my knees, but couldn't stand up because the plaza was whirling around me. Then, from some-where above, a voice called: "The President's dead! Long live the President! Long live Annalyn Court!"

Ragged cheering began and grew stronger, and they began to chant: "An-na-lyn! An-na-lyn! An-na-lyn!"

That's when I passed out.

23

I'VE BEEN IN THE MEDCEN FOR THE PAST TWO months. That's where I've been recording this.

The skin grafts are beginning to match the rest of me so I don't look all patches. The scars are fading. As one of the surgical techs said, "A laser can do a lot of damage."

I woke up in a dim room that smelled of medicine and roses. Here and there equipment lights glowed. I lay in a float bed, designed for treating burns. Only my head stuck out of the cocoon.

Across the room a window looked out on treetops and the shield beyond. Dots of light outside the shield were stars blurred by the crystal's distortion. The storm was over.

Remembering the storm brought back everything. At the thought of Evan, my tears blurred the lights. Hector was gone, and Shala. How could I still be alive?

Or was I?

I tucked down my head and peered into the neckline opening of my cocoon. No android body could ever look that disgusting. Where I think I was shot, there were five little boxlike things attached to me, with all sorts of tubes feeding into them. Rejuvenation units? The sound of a door opening behind me interrupted my viewing.

An older man and woman appeared at my bedside, wearing the bubble helmets required for a sterile environment. "I'm your chief physician and internist, Dr. Kibby," she said. "This is Dr. Polk, your burn specialist."

"You're healing well," he assured me. "The skin color will even out in time, the scars fade. You'll recover fully. Do you want to know the full extent of your injuries?"

I shook my head. Not after seeing those units on me.

"Is there anything you'd like to ask?" Dr. Kibby said when I just lay there mute. I hadn't talked for so long I was out of the habit.

"I was . . ." My voice broke. Clearing my throat, I started over and still didn't sound normal. "I . . . did you find anything *odd* in my brain?"

They exchanged glances and my hands went cold with fear.

"Yes." Dr. Kibby hesitated. "A foreign body. Too deep to be removed. We believe it to be a mind-transfer device. Do you know what that is?"

"Yes." I wondered if I should show them the little boomerang-shaped thing I'd found in the *Capri*'s hold.

"It doesn't appear to be working."

"There was no measurable radiation," Dr. Polk explained. "But we know so little about MT implants that it's hard to say."

"Would I know if it quit working?" I told them about the flash of lightning inside my head that day in the VIP lounge. "Could that have been it?"

"It's possible," said Dr. Kibby. "Did you feel discomfort?"

"I think I fainted—but I was very tired."

"Do you want it to be *off?*"

"Yes! It's like thinking you're going to turn into a vampire. Dead but immortal."

That answer seemed to please them; they both smiled at me. "Somewhere there must be experts on the subject. We'll find them for you," Dr. Kibby promised.

"We weren't aware that young people . . . that this procedure had been done in the past century," Dr. Polk said. "Have you had this since infancy?"

"I think so."

"Do you know who did the surgery?"

"No."

"Are there others like you?"

"Not many."

"Do you know who they are?"

"No." I suddenly was wary of their intense interest. "Where's the President?"

"He's dead. Remember?" Dr. Polk prompted as if speaking to a child. "He was struck by lightning—"

"I know he exploded," I said impatiently, "but that doesn't mean anything. He's an android—"

"Annalyn. Think! He blew up in public! People were struck by flying debris. Three onlookers filmed the whole scene on the plaza. He's finished. No matter how many copies he might have, they're useless."

"Not with a different face and a new ID."

"Then he couldn't be President," Dr. Polk reminded me.

"Not right away," I said, "but—"

"Not ever," Dr. Kibby said. "Some things have changed since you've been in here."

"Like what?"

"Androids have been outlawed on Mars," he said. "Probably as a result of that law, all Council members and the mayors of most of the major cities left our world—"

"Let's save some news for our next visit," Dr. Kibby interrupted. She was reading the dials at the head of my bed. "We've talked too long now."

"If the President's gone, who took his place? Evan?"

"Evan who?" Dr. Kibby's question gave me a much-needed sense of perspective.

"We have an adequate interim government," Dr. Polk assured me. "Don't worry about anything now. You must rest. The quicker you heal, the sooner you get out of here."

"Just one more question? Where did they put Hector?"

At that, their faces brightened. "We should have told you sooner—Hector will be fine," Dr. Kibby said. "He's being repaired. His outer housing took most of the damage—"

"He was shipped back to the manufacturer in one of the habitats," added Dr. Polk, "as soon as weather permitted. If we don't get another sandstorm, he should return in a month."

I started to cry again, from happiness this time, but the total care monitor didn't know that and put me back to sleep.

For the next two weeks I saw only medical personnel. No visitors allowed. "Visitors mean stress. Stress jeopardizes the immune system, slowing healing," I was told. It was just as well. I wasn't up to socializing. And I looked terrible.

Even my entertainment fare was "no stress." No newscasts. No controversy. Only classical music or ballet or travel and nature documentaries from Earth. I slept a lot.

That's when I started this. But even then I didn't know how it was going to end.

My first visitor was a lawyer from the firm that managed the President's personal estate. "Your doctors are allowing me only a few minutes of your time," he said, "but we felt it vital to inform you that your late father, the President, wished you to be his primary beneficiary. Unfortunately, his wife, Janis, demanded to see a copy of his will the day after his—ah—accident and is contesting the will—along with her son and several other family members."

My first reaction was a childish: *He did care.* And then my scars reminded me of reality. "If I had died before him—who would inherit my share then? Who's next in line?"

He flipped open his screen to consult the file and seemed surprised by what he read there. "That's odd. A second cousin, Reynolds Matthews. I would have thought—"

"Where does Reynolds Matthews live?"

"His last address is on Earth."

And that was how I learned where to start hunting for the immortal President's next android persona.

"Where are Evan and Janis Parker?"

"Currently en route to Earth. Antarctica, I believe. The son is to be married there and plans a long wedding tour."

As a result of the attorney's visit I quickly changed my own will. If I do inherit that enormous wealth, most of it will go to a charitable trust to buy property for the commoners of Midtown. That will keep the President from regaining it, under any name.

General Offrey was my first friendly visitor. I was up and walking by then. It was he who told me there had been a worldwide election. "We had to do it," he said. "We were left without a federal government. They work out of the Civic Center auditorium for now, until—"

"Who's our new President?"

"You are."

I laughed, thinking he was joking. He wasn't.

"How did you know I was going to recover?"

"We didn't," he admitted. "But we elected a very able Vice-President, Kami Ivanov. She's running things for now."

"But why me? I wouldn't have voted for a daughter of the old President. I could understand it if only Midtown voted. At least they know me."

"It was Midtown's enthusiasm for you, their tireless

campaigning on your behalf, that convinced the rest of Mars of your ability. You're quite a hero here.'' Then he smiled rather cynically and added, ''The fact that the President tried to kill you did a lot for your image.''

People seem to have more confidence in me than I have. I don't even know if I can do the job. I'll have to educate myself quickly on so many things. The good thing is, my term is only three Martian years. Council members are limited to a single five-year term.

Our new Council members come from all over Mars and Phobos. Only seven are from the elite class. All thirty-five were scanned to make sure none were androids.

That's another thing that's changed. MTs and androids are no longer a secret. Extreme longevity can't be explained away by ''rejuvenation.'' After seeing their President explode, it occurred to people there might be others like him. And they hunted for them. That's what prompted all the old Council members and half of the elite to leave Mars—most by private shuttle.

By popular demand, the new Council passed emergency laws outlawing androids on Mars. Their property was confiscated and is being held in trust. Equipment was installed at all spaceports to scan incoming passengers. Androids are refused entry.

I seem to be destined to start each new phase of my life by cleaning and tidying. When I get out of here, my first big problem will concern androids. Unlike most people, I'm not sure we should deny them all civil rights. But then, I'm not sure we shouldn't.

As for MTs, like myself and Evan and who knows

how many others, we'll have to wait until the surgeons who did those implants are found. I suspect the work was done by android surgeons—leftovers from the early days of Mars who are now in hiding.

And where do we begin to search for our minds' copies, if they still exist? They must be hidden somewhere on Mars, maybe in one of the factories, or down there in those ghostly suites where the pioneers lived.

I hope Hector comes home soon. It's very lonely here without him.

That sounds pathetic, being lonely for a robot. But it's true. The thing is, with Shala gone, I don't have any real friends. And knowing Evan has been a thorough education in what false friends can be.

So while I'm the President, it won't be wise to trust anyone who wants to become my friend. Power, like lasers, can do a lot of damage.

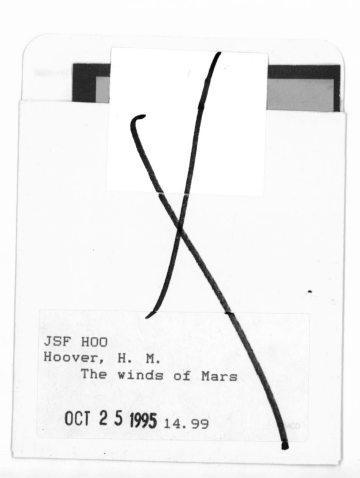

JSF HOO
Hoover, H. M.
     The winds of Mars

OCT 2 5 1995 14.99